ROGUE, PRISONER

(OF CROWNS AND GLORY—BOOK 2)

MORGAN RICE

Books by Morgan Rice

THE WAY OF STEEL
ONLY THE WORTHY (BOOK #1)

VAMPIRE, FALLEN
BEFORE DAWN (BOOK #1)

OF CROWNS AND GLORY
SLAVE, WARRIOR, QUEEN (BOOK #1)
ROGUE, PRISONER, PRINCESS (BOOK #2)

KINGS AND SORCERERS
RISE OF THE DRAGONS
RISE OF THE VALIANT
THE WEIGHT OF HONOR
A FORGE OF VALOR
A REALM OF SHADOWS
NIGHT OF THE BOLD

THE SORCERER'S RING
A QUEST OF HEROES
A MARCH OF KINGS
A FATE OF DRAGONS
A CRY OF HONOR
A VOW OF GLORY
A CHARGE OF VALOR
A RITE OF SWORDS
A GRANT OF ARMS
A SKY OF SPELLS
A SEA OF SHIELDS
A REIGN OF STEEL
A LAND OF FIRE
A RULE OF QUEENS
AN OATH OF BROTHERS
A DREAM OF MORTALS
A JOUST OF KNIGHTS
THE GIFT OF BATTLE

THE SURVIVAL TRILOGY
ARENA ONE (Book #1)
ARENA TWO (Book #2)
ARENA THREE (Book #3)

the Vampire Journals
turned (book #1)
loved (book #2)
betrayed (book #3)
destined (book #4)
desired (book #5)
betrothed (book #6)
vowed (book #7)
found (book #8)
resurrected (book #9)
craved (book #10)
fated (book #11)
obsessed (book#12)

CHAPTER ONE

"Ceres! Ceres! Ceres!"

Ceres could feel the chant of the crowd as clearly as her own thudding heartbeat. She raised her sword in acknowledgment, tightening her grip as she did, testing the leather. It didn't matter to her that they'd probably only learned her name a few moments ago. It was enough that they knew it, and that it was reverberating through her, so that she could feel it almost as a physical force.

Across the Stade, facing her, her opponent, the massive combatlord, paced the sands. Ceres swallowed at the sight of him, fear rising up in her, as much as she tried to suppress it. This, she knew, could very well be the last fight of her life.

The combatlord paced like a caged lion, swinging his sword through the air in arcs that seemed to be designed to show off his bulging muscles. With his breastplate and visored helmet, he looked as if he could have been carved from stone. It was hard for Ceres to believe that he was just flesh and blood.

Ceres closed her eyes and steeled herself.

You can do this, she told herself. *You may not win, but you must face him valiantly. If you are to die, you must die with honor.*

A trumpet blast rang in Ceres's ears, rising up even over the baying of the crowd. It filled the arena, and suddenly, her opponent was charging.

He was faster than she thought such a big man had any right to be, on her before she had a chance to react. It was all Ceres could do to dodge, kicking up dust as she got out of the warrior's path.

The combatlord swung his blade with two hands and Ceres ducked, feeling the rush of air as it passed. He hacked down like a butcher wielding a cleaver, and when she spun and blocked the stroke, the impact of metal on metal rang up her arms. She did not think it possible a warrior could be that strong.

She circled away, her opponent following with a grim inevitability.

Ceres heard her name mixed in with the cheers and boos of the crowd. She forced herself to stay focused; she kept her eyes fixed on her opponent and tried to remember her training, thinking through all the things that might happen next. She tried to slash, and then rolled her wrist to send her sword around the parry.

But the combatlord merely grunted as her blade took a nick out of his forearm.

He smiled as if he'd enjoyed it.

1

"You'll pay for that," he warned. His accent was thick, from one of the far corners of the Empire.

He was on her again, forcing her to parry and dodge, and she knew she couldn't risk a head-on clash, not with someone this strong.

Ceres felt the ground give way beneath her right foot, a sensation of emptiness there where there should have been firm support. She glanced down and saw sand pouring down into a pit below. For a moment, her foot hung over empty space, and she thrust out blindly with her sword as she struggled to keep her balance.

The combatlord's parry was almost contemptuous. For an instant, Ceres was sure she was going to die, because there was no way to fully stop the answering stroke. She felt the jarring impact of the blow against her blade. It only slowed it, though, as it slammed into her armor. Her breastplate pressed back into her flesh with bruising force, while at the spot where it ended, she felt pain flare white hot as the sword cut along her collarbone.

She stumbled back and as she did, she saw more pits opening around the floor of the arena, like the mouths of hungry beasts. And then, desperate, she had an idea: maybe she could use them to her advantage.

Ceres skirted around the edges of the pits, hoping to slow his approach.

"Ceres!" Paulo called.

She turned and her weapon-keeper threw a short spear in her direction. Its shaft thudded into her slick palm as she caught it, the wood feeling rough. The spear was shorter than might have been used in a real battle, but it was still long enough to thrust its leaf-shaped head across the pits.

"I'll take you a slice at a time," the combatlord promised, edging his way around.

With an opponent this strong, Ceres thought, her best hope was to try to wear him down. How long could someone that huge keep fighting? Already, Ceres could feel the burn of her own muscles, and the sweat that dripped down her face. How much worse would it be for the combatlord she faced?

It was impossible to know for sure, but it had to be her best hope. So she dodged and she jabbed, using the length of the spear as best she could. She managed to slip through the massive warrior's defenses, yet still, it only clattered off his armor.

The combatlord kicked up dust towards Ceres's eyes, but she turned away in time. She spun back and swept the spear low,

2

toward his unprotected legs. He jumped clear of that sweep, but she managed to slice another wound along his forearm as she drew the spear back.

Ceres jabbed low and high now, aiming for her opponent's limbs. The big man parried and blocked, trying to find a way past the probing point, but Ceres kept it moving. She jabbed it in toward his face, hoping to at least distract him.

The combatlord caught the spear. He grabbed it behind the head, yanking it forward as he stepped aside. Ceres had to let go, because she didn't want to risk being pulled onto the big man's sword. Her opponent snapped the spear across his knee as easily as he might have broken a twig.

The crowd roared.

Ceres felt a cold sweat up her back. For an instant, she had the image of the big man breaking her body as easily. She swallowed at the thought and readied her sword again.

She grabbed the hilt with both hands as the next blows came, because it was the only way to absorb some of the power of the combatlord's attacks. Even so, it was impossibly hard. Every blow felt like she was a bell being hit by a hammer. Every one sent shockwaves running through her arms.

Already, Ceres could feel herself tiring under the assault. Every breath came ragged, feeling like she dragged it in by force. There was no question now of trying to counterattack, or do anything but step back and hope.

And then it happened. Slowly, Ceres felt the power welling up inside her. It came with a warmth, like the first embers of a brush fire. It sat in the pit of her belly, waiting for her, and Ceres reached for it.

Energy flooded through her. The world slowed, moving at a crawl, and she suddenly felt she had all the time in the world to parry the next attack.

She had all the strength, too. She blocked it easily and then swung her sword around and slashed the combatlord's arm in a blur of light and speed.

"Ceres! Ceres!" the crowd roared.

She saw the combatlord's rage growing as the crowd's chanting continued. She could understand why. They were meant to be chanting for *him*, proclaiming his victory, enjoying her death.

He bellowed and charged forward. Ceres waited as long as she dared, forcing herself to stay still until he nearly reached her.

Then she dropped. She felt the whisper of his blade passing over her head, then the rough sand as her knees touched down. She threw herself forward, swinging her sword around in an arc that slammed into the combatlord's legs as he passed.

He tumbled face first, his sword spilling from his hand.

The crowd went wild.

Ceres stood over him, looking at the awful ruin her sword had made of his legs. For a moment, she wondered if he might manage to stand even like that, but he collapsed back, turning to his back and lifting one hand as he begged for mercy. Ceres held back, looking around for the royals who would decide if the man in front of her lived or died. Either way, she resolved, she would not kill a helpless warrior.

Another trumpet blast came.

A roar followed it as the iron gates at the side of the arena opened, and the tone of it was enough to send a shiver through Ceres. In that moment, she felt like nothing more than prey, something to be hunted, something that had to run. She dared a glance up toward the royal enclosure, knowing this had to be deliberate. The fight had been over. She'd *won*. That wasn't good enough, though. They were going to kill her, she realized, one way or another. They would not let her leave the Stade alive.

A creature lumbered in, larger than a human, covered in shaggy fur. Fangs stuck out from a bearlike face, while spiny protrusions stuck out along the creature's back. Its feet held claws the length of daggers. Ceres didn't know what it was, but she didn't need to in order to know that it would be deadly.

The bear-like creature sank to all fours and ran forward, while Ceres readied her sword.

It reached the fallen combatlord first, and Ceres would have looked away if she'd dared. The man cried out as it pounced, but there was no way he could roll out of the way in time. Those giant paws smashed down, and Ceres heard the crunch of his breastplate giving way. The beast roared as it savaged her former opponent.

When it looked up, its fangs were wet with blood. It looked at Ceres, bared its teeth, and charged.

She barely managed to step aside in time, slashing with her sword as it passed. The creature gave a bellow of pain.

Yet sheer momentum tore the blade from her hands, feeling as though it would tear her arm away if she didn't let go. She watched with horror as her blade spun across the sand and into one of the pits.

The beast continued to advance, and Ceres, frantic, glanced down at the spot where the two broken sections of spear lay on the

4

sand. She dove for them, grabbing a section and rolling in one movement.

As she rose to one knee, the creature was already charging. She couldn't run, she told herself. This was her only chance.

It slammed into her, the weight and speed of the thing lifting Ceres from her feet. There was no time to think, no time to be afraid. She thrust with the broken section of spear, striking with it again and again as the bear-beast's paws closed in on her.

Its strength was terrible, far too much to match. Ceres felt as though her ribs might burst with the pressure of it, the breastplate she wore creaking under the creature's strength. She felt its claws raking at her back and legs, agony searing across her.

Its hide was too thick. Ceres struck again and again, but she could feel the tip of the spear barely penetrating its flesh while it tore at her, its claws ripping across any exposed skin.

Ceres closed her eyes. With all she had, she reached for the power within her, not even knowing if it would work.

She felt herself surge with a ball of power. She then threw all her force into her spear, thrusting it up into the space where she hoped the creature's heart would be.

The beast shrieked as it reared back away from her.

The crowd roared.

Ceres, smarting from the pain of its scratches, scrambled out from under it and stood weakly. She looked down as the beast, the spear lodged in its heart, rolled and whined, making a sound that seemed far too small for something so large.

Then it stiffened, and died.

"Ceres! Ceres! Ceres!"

The Stade filled with cheers again. Everywhere Ceres looked, there were people calling out her name. Nobles and ordinary folk alike seemed to be joining in the chanting, losing themselves in that one moment of her victory.

"Ceres! Ceres! Ceres!"

She found herself drinking it in. It was impossible not to be caught up in the feeling of adulation. Her whole body seemed to pulse in time with the chanting that surrounded her and she spread her hands as if to welcome it all in. She turned in a slow circle, watching the faces of those who hadn't even heard of her a day ago, but who were now treating her as though she was the only person in the world who mattered.

Ceres was so caught up in that moment that she barely even felt the pain of the wounds she'd suffered anymore. Her shoulder hurt

5

now, so she touched a hand to it. It came away wet, although her blood was still bright red in the sunlight.

Ceres stared at that stain for several seconds. The crowd was still chanting her name, but the pounding of her heart in her ears suddenly seemed far louder. She looked up at the crowd, and it took her a moment to realize that she was doing it from her knees. She couldn't remember falling to them.

From the corner of her eye, Ceres could see Paulo hurrying forward, but that seemed far too distant, as if it had nothing to do with her. Blood dripped from her fingers to the sand, darkening it where it touched. She had never felt so dizzy, so light-headed.

And the last thing she knew she was already falling, face-first, toward the floor of the arena, unable, she felt, to ever move again.

CHAPTER TWO

Thanos slowly opened his eyes, confused as he felt waves lapping at his ankles, his wrists. Beneath him, he could feel the gritty white sand of Haylon's beaches. Salt spray occasionally filled his mouth, making it hard to breathe.

Thanos looked out sideways along the beach, unable to do more than that. Even that was a struggle, as he drifted in and out of consciousness. In the distance, he thought he could make out flames and the sounds of violence. Screams came to him, along with the sound of steel clashing on steel.

The island, he remembered. *Haylon. Their attack had begun.*

So why was he lying on the sand?

It took a moment for the pain in his shoulder to answer that question. He remembered, and winced at the memory. He remembered the moment the sword had plunged into him, lancing into his upper back from behind. He remembered the shock of it as the Typhoon had betrayed him.

The pain burned through Thanos, expanding like a flower from the wound in his back. Every breath hurt. He tried to lift his head— but he only blacked out.

The next time Thanos woke, he was face-down on the sand again, and he was only able to tell that time had passed because the tide had risen a little, the water lapping at his waist now rather than his ankles. He was finally able to lift his head enough to see that there were other bodies on the beach. The dead seemed to cover the world, stretched out on the white beaches as far as he could see. He saw men in the armor of the Empire, sprawled where they had fallen, mixed in with the defenders who had died protecting their home.

The stench of death filled Thanos's nostrils, and it was all he could do not to throw up. No one had sorted the dead into friend and foe yet. Such niceties could wait until after the battle was done. Perhaps the Empire would leave it for the tide to do; a glance behind showed blood in the water, and Thanos could see the fins breaking through the waves. Not large sharks yet, scavengers rather than hunters—but how large would they need to be in order to devour him when the tide rose?

Thanos felt a wave of panic. He tried to haul himself up the beach, pulling with his arms as though trying to climb across the sand. He cried out in pain as he pulled himself forward, perhaps half the length of his body.

7

Blackness swam in his vision again.

When he came to, Thanos was on his side, looking up at figures who squatted over him, close enough that he could have reached out for them if he'd had the strength left to do it. They didn't look like soldiers of the Empire, didn't really look like soldiers at all, and Thanos had spent long enough around warriors to know the difference. These, a younger man and an older, looked more like farmers, ordinary men who had probably fled their homes to avoid the violence. That didn't mean they were less dangerous, though. Both held knives, and Thanos found himself wondering if they might be as much scavengers as the sharks. He knew there were always those looking to rob the dead after battles.

"This one's still breathing," the first of them said.

"I can see that. Just cut his throat and be done with it."

Thanos tensed, his body getting ready to fight even though there was nothing he could have done then.

"Look at him," the younger man insisted. "Someone stabbed him in the back."

Thanos saw the older man frown slightly at that. He moved around behind Thanos, out of his line of sight. Thanos managed to keep from crying out again as the man touched the spot where blood still flowed from the wound. He was a prince of the Empire. He wasn't going to show weakness.

"Looks like you're right. Help me get him up where the sharks won't get him. The others will want to see this."

Thanos saw the younger man nod, and together, they managed to lift him, armor and all. This time, Thanos did cry out, unable to stop the pain as they pulled him up over the beach.

They left him like driftwood, past the point where the tide had left seaweed behind, abandoning him on the dry sand. They hurried away, but Thanos was too caught up in the pain to watch them go.

There was no way for him to gauge the time that passed then. He could still hear the battle in the background, with its cries of violence and anger, its rallying cries and its signal horns. A battle could last minutes or hours, though. It could be over in the first rush, or keep going until neither side had the strength to do more than stumble away. Thanos had no way of knowing which this was.

Eventually, a group of men approached. These *did* look like soldiers, with that harder edge that only came to a man once he'd fought for his life. It was easy to see which of them was the leader. The tall, dark-haired man at the front didn't wear the elaborately worked armor that a general of the Empire might have, but everyone there looked to him as the group approached, obviously awaiting orders.

The newcomer was probably in his thirties, with a short beard as dark as the rest of his hair, and a spare frame that nevertheless held a sense of strength. He wore a short, stabbing sword on each hip, and Thanos guessed that it wasn't just for show, judging by the way his hands hovered next to the hilts automatically. His expression seemed to Thanos to be silently calculating every angle present on the beach, watching out for the possibility of an ambush, always thinking ahead. His eyes locked on to Thanos's, and the smile that followed had a strange kind of humor behind it, as though its owner had seen something in the world that no one else had.

"This is what you two have brought me out here to see?" he said, as the two who had found Thanos stepped forward. "One dying Imperial soldier in armor too shiny for his own good?"

"A noble though," the older one said. "You can see that by the armor."

"And he's been stabbed in the back," the younger pointed out. "By his own men, it seems."

"So he's not even good enough for the scum who are trying to take our island?" the leader said.

Thanos watched as the man moved closer, kneeling beside him. Maybe he intended to finish what the Typhoon had started. No soldier of Haylon would have any love for those on his side of the conflict.

"What did you do that your own side would try to kill you?" the newcomer asked, quietly enough that only Thanos could hear him.

Thanos managed to find the strength to shake his head. "I don't know." The words came out cracked and broken. Even if he hadn't been wounded, he'd been lying on the sand a long time. "But I didn't want this. I didn't want to fight here."

That earned another of those strange smiles that seemed to Thanos to be laughing at the world even though there was nothing to laugh at.

"And yet here you are," the newcomer said. "You didn't want to take part in an invasion, but you're on our beaches, rather than safe at home. You didn't want to offer us violence, but the Empire's army is burning homes as we speak. Do you know what's happening up that beach?"

Thanos shook his head. Even that hurt.

"We're losing," the man continued. "Oh, we're fighting hard enough, but that doesn't matter. Not with odds like this. The battle

9

still rages, but that's just because half of my side are too stubborn to recognize the truth. We don't have enough time for distractions like this."

Thanos watched as the newcomer drew one of his swords. It looked wickedly sharp. So sharp that he probably wouldn't even feel it as it plunged into his heart. Instead, though, the other man gestured with it.

"*You* and *you*," he said to the men, "bring our new friend. Perhaps he's worth something to the other side." He grinned. "And if he's not, I shall kill him myself."

The last thing Thanos felt were strong hands gripping him under his arms, yanking him up, dragging him away, before he finally lapsed back into darkness.

CHAPTER THREE

Berin felt the ache of longing as he trekked along the route home to Delos, the only thing keeping him going, thoughts of his family—of Ceres. The thought of returning to his daughter was enough to make him press on, even though he'd found the days of walking tough, the roads beneath his feet rough with ruts and stones. His bones were not getting any younger, and already he could feel his knee aching from the journey, adding to the pains that came from a life of hammering and heating metal.

It was all worth it, though, to see home again, though. To see his family. All the time he'd been away, it was all Berin had wanted. He could picture it now. Marita would be cooking in the back of the humble wooden home, the scent of it wafting out past the front door. Sartes would be playing somewhere around the back, probably with Nasos watching him, even if his older son would be pretending that he wasn't.

And then there would be Ceres. He loved all his children, but with Ceres there had always been that extra connection. She had been the one to help out around his forge, the one who had taken after him most, and who seemed the most likely to follow in his footsteps. Leaving Marita and the boys had been a painful duty, necessary if he was to provide for his family. Leaving Ceres behind had felt as though he'd abandoned some part of himself when he left.

Now it was time to reclaim it.

Berin only wished he brought happier news. He walked along the gravel track that led back to their house, and he frowned; it wasn't winter yet, but it would be soon enough. The plan had been for him to leave and find work. Lords always needed bladesmiths to provide weapons for their guards, their wars, their Killings. Yet it turned out that they didn't need *him*. They had their own men. Younger, stronger men. Even the king who had seemed to want his work had turned out to want Berin as he had been ten years ago.

The thought hurt, yet he knew he should have guessed that they would have no need for a man with more gray in his beard than black.

It would have hurt more if it hadn't meant that he got to go home. Home was the thing that mattered for Berin, even when it was little more than a square of rough-sawn wooden walls, topped with a turf roof. Home was about the people waiting there, and the thought of them was enough to make him quicken his steps.

11

As he crested a hill, though, and the first view of it came, Bering knew that something was wrong. His stomach plunged. Berin knew what home felt like. For all the barrenness of the surrounding land, home was a place filled with life. There was always noise there, whether it was joyful or argumentative. At this time of year too, there would always have been at least a few crops growing in the plot around it, vegetables and small berry bushes, hardy things that always produced at least something to feed them.

That was not what he saw before him.

Berin broke into as much of a run then as he could manage after so long a walk, the sense of something wrong gnawing away at him, feeling like one of his vises clamped around his heart.

He reached the door and threw it wide. Maybe, he thought, everything would be all right. Maybe they had spotted him and were all just ensuring that his arrival would be a surprise.

It was dim inside, the windows crusted with grime. And there, a presence.

Marita stood in the main room, stirring a pot that smelled too sour to Berin. She turned toward him as he burst in, and as she did, Berin knew he'd been right. Something was wrong. Something was very wrong.

"Marita?" he began.

"Husband." Even the flat way she said that told him that nothing was as it should be. Any other time he'd been away, Marita had thrown her arms around him as he'd come in the door. She'd always seemed full of life. Now, she seemed…empty.

"What's going on here?" Berin asked.

"I don't know what you mean." Again, there was less emotion than there should have been, as though something in his wife had broken, letting all the joy out of her.

"Why is everything around here so… so *still*?" Berin demanded. "Where are our children?"

"They aren't here right now," Marita said. She moved back to the pot as though everything was perfectly normal.

"Where are they, then?" Berin wasn't going to let it go. He could believe that the boys might have run down to the nearest stream or had errands to run, but one of his children at least would have seen him coming home and been there to meet him. "Where is Ceres?"

"Oh yes," Marita said, and Berin could hear the bitterness there now. "Of course you would ask after *her*. Not how things are with me. Not your sons. Her."

Berin had never heard his wife sound quite like this before. Oh, he'd always known there was something hard in Marita, more concerned for herself than for the rest of the world, but now it sounded as though her heart was ashes.

Marita seemed to calm down then, and the sheer speed with which she did it made it suspicious to Berin.

"You want to know what your precious daughter did?" she said. "She ran away."

Berin's apprehension deepened. He shook his head. "I don't believe that."

Marita kept going. "She ran away. Didn't say where she was going, just stole what she could from us when she left."

"We have no money to steal," Berin said. "And Ceres would never do that."

"Of course you'll take her side," Marita said. "But she took… things from around here, possessions. Anything she thought she could sell in the next town, knowing that girl. She abandoned us."

If that was what Marita thought, then Berin was sure she'd never really known her daughter. Or him, if she thought he would believe such an obvious lie. He took her shoulders in his hands, and even though he didn't possess all the strength he'd once had, Berin was still strong enough so that his wife felt fragile by comparison.

"Tell me the truth, Marita! What's happened here?" Berin shook her, as if somehow that might jolt the old version of her back into being, and she might suddenly return to being the Marita he'd married all those years before. All it did was make her pull away.

"Your boys are dead!" Marita yelled back. The words filled the small space of their home, coming out in a snarl. Her voice dropped. "That's what's happened. Our sons are dead."

The words hit Berin like a kick from a horse that didn't want shoeing. "No," he said. "It's another lie. It has to be."

He couldn't think of another thing Marita could have said that would have hurt as much. She had to be just saying this to hurt him.

"When did you decide that you hated me so much?" Berin asked, because that was the only reason he could think of that his wife would throw something so vile at him, using the idea of their sons' deaths as a weapon.

Now Berin could see tears in Marita's eyes. There hadn't been any when she'd been talking about their daughter supposedly running away.

"When you decided to abandon us," his wife snapped back. "When I had to watch Nasos die!"

"Just Nasos?" Berin said.

"Isn't that enough?" Marita shouted back. "Or don't you care about your sons?"

"A moment ago you said that Sartes was dead too," Berin said. "Stop lying to me, Marita!"

"Sartes is dead too," his wife insisted. "Soldiers came and took him. They dragged him off to be a part of the Empire's army, and he's just a boy. How long do you think he will survive as a part of that? No, both of my boys are gone, while Ceres…"

"What?" Berin demanded.

Marita just shook her head. "If you'd been here, it might not even have happened."

"*You* were here," Berin spat back, trembling all over. "That had been the point. You think I wanted to go? You were meant to look after them while I found the money for us to eat."

Despair gripped Berin then, and he could feel himself starting to weep, as he hadn't wept since he was a child. His oldest son was dead. For all the other lies Marita had come out with, that sounded like the truth. The loss left a hole that seemed to be impossible to fill, even with the grief and anger that were welling up inside him. He forced himself to focus on the others, because it seemed like the only way to stop it from overwhelming him.

"Soldiers took Sartes?" he asked. "Imperial soldiers?"

"You think I'm lying to you about that?" Marita asked.

"I don't know what to believe anymore," Berin replied. "You didn't even try to stop them?"

"They held a knife to my throat," Marita said. "I had to."

"You had to do what?" Berin asked.

Marita shook her head. "I had to call him outside. They would have killed me."

"So you gave him to them instead?"

"What do you think I could do?" Marita demanded. "You weren't here."

And Berin would probably feel guilty about that for as long as he lived. Marita was right. Maybe if he had been here, this wouldn't have happened. He'd gone off, looking to keep his family from starving, and while he'd been away, things had fallen apart. Feeling guilty didn't replace the grief or the anger, though. It only added to it. It bubbled inside Berin, feeling like something alive and fighting to get out.

"What about Ceres?" he demanded. He shook Marita again. "Tell me! The truth this time. What did you do?"

Marita just pulled away again though, and this time she sank down on her haunches on the floor, curling up and not even looking at him. "Find out for yourself. I've been the one who's had to live with this. Me, not you."

There was a part of Berin that wanted to keep shaking her until she gave him an answer. That wanted to force the truth from her, whatever it took. Yet he wasn't that kind of man, and knew he never could be. Even the thought of it disgusted him.

He didn't take anything from the house when he left. There wasn't anything he wanted there. As he looked back at Marita, so totally wrapped up in her own bitterness that she'd given up her son, tried to disguise what had happened to their children, it was hard to believe that there had ever been.

Berin stepped out into the open air, blinking away what was left of his tears. It was only when the brightness of the sun hit him that he realized he had no idea what he was going to do next. What could he do? There was no helping his oldest son, not now, while the others could be anywhere.

"That doesn't matter," Berin told himself. He could feel the determination within him turning into something like the iron he worked. "It won't stop me."

Perhaps someone nearby would have seen where they had gone. Certainly, someone would know where the army was, and Berin knew as well as anyone that a man who made blades could always find a way to get closer to the army.

As for Ceres... there would be something. She must be *somewhere*. Because the alternative was unthinkable.

Berin looked out over the countryside surrounding his home. Ceres was out there somewhere. So was Sartes. He said the next words aloud, because doing that seemed to turn it into a promise, to himself, to the world, to his children.

"I'll find you both," he vowed. "Whatever it takes."

CHAPTER FOUR

Breathing hard, Sartes ran among the army's tents, clutching the scroll in his hand and wiping the sweat from his eyes, knowing that if he did not reach his commander's tent soon he would be flogged. He ducked and weaved as best he could, knowing his time was running out. He had been held up far too many times already.

Sartes already had burn marks on his shins from the times he'd gotten it wrong, their sting just one more among many by now. He blinked, desperate, looking around the army camp, trying to make out the correct direction to run among the endless grid of tents. There were signs and standards there to mark the way, but he was still trying to learn their pattern.

Sartes felt something catch his foot, and then he was tumbling, the world seeming to turn upside down as he fell. For a moment he thought he'd tripped on a rope, but then he looked up to see soldiers laughing. The one at their head was an older man, with stubble-short hair turning gray and scars from too many battles.

Fear filled Sartes then, but also a kind of resignation; this was just life in the army for a conscript like him. He didn't demand to know why the other man had done it, because saying anything was a sure way to a beating. As far as he could see, practically anything was.

Instead, he stood up, brushing away the worst of the mud from his tunic.

"What are you about, whelp?" the soldier who'd tripped him demanded.

"Running an errand for my commander, sir," Sartes said, lifting a scrap of parchment for the other man to see. He hoped it would be enough to keep him safe. Often it wasn't, in spite of the rules that said orders took precedence over anything else.

In the time since he'd arrived there, Sartes had learned that the Imperial army had plenty of rules. Some were official: leave the camp without permission, refuse to follow orders, betray the army, and you could be killed. March the wrong way, do anything without permission, and you could be beaten. There were other rules too, though. Less official ones that could be just as dangerous to break.

"What errand would that be?" the soldier demanded. Others were gathering around now. The army was always short of sources of entertainment, so if there was the prospect of a little fun at a conscript's expense, people paid attention.

Sartes did his best to look apologetic. "I don't know, sir. I just have orders to deliver this message. You can read it if you like."

That was a calculated risk. Most of the ordinary soldiers couldn't read. He hoped that the tone of it wouldn't earn him a cuff around the ear for insubordination, but tried not to show any fear. Not showing fear was one of the rules that wasn't written down. The army had at least as many of those rules as official ones. Rules about who you had to know to get better food. About who knew whom, and who you had to be careful of, regardless of rank. Knowing them seemed to be the only way to survive.

"Well, you'd better get on with it then!" the soldier roared, aiming a kick at Sartes to get him moving. The others there laughed as if it was the greatest joke they'd seen.

One of the biggest unwritten rules seemed to be that the new conscripts were fair game. Since he'd arrived, Sartes had been punched and slapped, beaten and shoved. He'd been made to run until he felt like collapsing, then run some more. He'd been laden with so much gear that he'd felt as though he could barely stand up, made to carry it, to dig holes in the ground for no apparent reason, to work. He'd heard stories of men in the ranks who liked to do worse to the new conscripts. Even if they died, what did it matter to the army? They were there to be thrown at the enemy. Everyone expected them to die.

Sartes had expected to die the first day. By the end of it, he'd even felt as though he wanted to. He'd curled up inside the too thin tent they'd assigned him and shivered, hoping that the ground would swallow him up. Impossibly, the next day had been worse. Another new conscript, whose name Sartes hadn't even learned, had been killed that day. He'd been caught trying to run away, and they'd all had to watch his execution, as if it were some kind of lesson. The only lesson Sartes had been able to see was how cruel the army was to anyone who let it see that they were afraid. That was when he'd started trying to bury his fear, not showing it even though it was there in the background almost every moment he was awake.

He made a detour between the tents now, switching directions briefly to swing by one of the mess tents, where a day ago, one of the cooks had needed help composing a message home. The army barely fed its conscripts, and Sartes could feel his stomach rumbling at the prospect of food, but he didn't eat what he took with him as he ran for his commanding officer's tent.

"Where have you been?" the officer demanded. His tone made it clear that being slowed down by other soldiers wouldn't count as an excuse. But then, Sartes had known that. It was part of why he'd gone to the mess tent.

"Collecting this on the way, sir," Sartes said, holding out the apple tart that he'd heard was the officer's favorite. "I knew that there might not be an opportunity for you to get it yourself today."

The officer's demeanor changed instantly. "That's very thoughtful, conscript—"

"Sartes, sir." Sartes didn't dare to smile.

"Sartes. We could use some soldiers who know how to think. Although next time, remember that the orders have to come first."

"Yes sir," Sartes said. "Is there anything you require me to do, sir?"

The officer waved him away. "Not right now, but I'll remember your name. Dismissed."

Sartes left the commander's pavilion feeling a lot better than when he'd gone in. He hadn't been sure that the small act would be enough to save him after the delay the soldiers had caused. For now, though, he seemed to have avoided punishment, and had managed to get to the position where an officer knew who he was.

It felt like a knife edge, but the whole army felt like that to Sartes then. So far, he'd survived in the army by being clever, and keeping one step ahead of the worst of the violence there. He'd seen boys his age killed, or beaten so badly that it was obvious that they'd die soon. Even so, he wasn't sure how long he would be able to keep that up. For a conscript like him, this was the kind of place where violence and death could only be put off so long.

Sartes swallowed as he thought of all the things that could go wrong. A soldier might take a beating too far. An officer might take offense at any tiny action and order a punishment designed to deter the others with its cruelty. He might be pushed forward into battle at any moment, and he'd heard that conscripts went at the front of the line to "weed out the weak." Even training might prove deadly, when the army had little use for blunt weapons, and conscripts were given little real instruction.

The one fear that sat behind them all was that someone would find out he'd tried to join Rexus and the rebels. There should be no way that they could, but even the faintest possibility was enough to outweigh all the others. Sartes had seen the body of a soldier accused of having rebel sympathies. His own unit had been commanded to hack him to pieces to prove their loyalty. Sartes didn't want to end up like that. Just the thought of it was enough to make his stomach tighten over and above the hunger.

"You there!" a voice called, and Sartes started. It was impossible to shake the feeling that maybe someone had guessed what he was thinking. He forced himself to at least pretend to be calm. Sartes looked round to see a soldier in the elaborately muscled armor of a sergeant, with pockmarks on his cheeks so deep they were almost like another landscape. "You're the captain's messenger?"

"I've just come from carrying a message to him, sir," Sartes said. It wasn't quite a lie.

"Then you're good enough for me. Go find out where the carts with my timber supplies have gotten to. If anyone gives you trouble, tell them Venn sent you."

Sartes saluted hurriedly. "At once, sir."

He ran off on the errand, but as he went he did not focus on the mission at hand. He took a longer way, a more circuitous way. A way that would enable him to spy the camp's outskirts, their choke points, a way that would allow him to pry for any weak points.

Because, dead or not, Sartes would find a way to escape tonight.

CHAPTER FIVE

Lucious pushed his way through the crowds of nobles in the castle's throne room, fuming as he went. He fumed at the fact that he had to shove his way through, when everyone there should have stood aside and bowed down, making way for him. He fumed at the fact that Thanos was off getting all the glory, crushing the rebels on Haylon. Above all, though, he fumed at the way things had gone in the Stade. That wench Ceres had ruined his plans once again.

Ahead, Lucious could see the king and queen in deep conversation with Cosmas, the old fool from the library. Lucious had thought he'd seen the last of the aged scholar as a child, when they'd all been made to learn ludicrous facts about the world and its workings. But no, apparently, in the wake of the letter he had provided, showing Ceres's true treachery, Cosmas got to have the ear of his king.

Lucious kept pushing his way forward. Around him, he could hear the nobles of the court at their petty plotting. He could see his distant cousin Stephania not far away, laughing at some joke another perfectly presented noble girl had made. She looked over, catching Lucious's eye just long enough to smile at him. She really was, Lucious decided, quite an empty-headed thing. But a beautiful one. Perhaps in the future, he thought, there might be an opportunity to spend more time around the noble girl. He was at least as impressive as Thanos, by any estimation.

For now, though, Lucious's anger at what had happened was too great for even those thoughts to amuse him. He stalked to the foot of the thrones, right to the edge of the raised dais there.

"She still lives!" he blurted out as he neared the throne. It didn't matter to him that it was loud enough to carry to the whole room. Let them hear, he decided. It certainly made no difference that Cosmas was still whispering away to the king and queen. What, Lucious wondered, could a man who spent his time around scrolls possibly have that was worth saying?

"Did you hear me?" Lucious said. "The girl is—"

"Still alive, yes," the king said, stopping him with a hand held up for silence. "We are discussing more important matters. Thanos is missing in the battle for Haylon."

The gesture was just one more thing to add to Lucious's anger. He was being treated like some servant to be quieted, he thought. Even so, he waited. He couldn't afford the king's anger. Besides, it took a moment or two to digest what he'd just heard.

Thanos was missing? Lucious tried to work out how it affected him. Would it change his position within the court? He found himself glancing across at Stephania again, thoughtful.

"Thank you, Cosmas," the queen said at last.

Lucious watched as the scholar descended back into the crowd of watching nobles. Only then did the king and queen give him their attention. Lucious tried to stand straight. He would not let the others there see any of the resentment that burned through him at the small insult. If anyone else had treated him this way, Lucious told himself, he would have killed them by now.

"We are aware that Ceres survived the last Killing," King Claudius said. To Lucious, he barely even sounded annoyed by it, let alone as though he were burning with the same anger that flooded him at the thought of the peasant.

But then, Lucious thought, the king hadn't been the one who had been defeated by the girl. Not once, but twice now, because she'd bested him through some trickery when he'd gone to her room to teach her a lesson too. Lucious felt that he had every reason, every *right*, to take her survival personally.

"Then you're aware that it can't be allowed to continue," Lucious said. He couldn't keep his tone as courtly and even as it should be. "You must deal with her."

"Must?" Queen Athena said. "Careful, Lucious. We are still your rulers."

"With respect, your majesties," Stephania said, and Lucious watched her glide forward, her silk dress clinging to her. "Lucious is right. Ceres cannot be allowed to live."

Lucious saw the king's eyes narrow slightly.

"And what do you suggest we do?" King Claudius demanded. "Drag her out onto the sands and have her beheaded? You were the one who suggested that she should fight, Stephania. You can't complain if she isn't dying fast enough for your tastes."

Lucious understood that part, at least. There was no pretext for her death, and the people seemed to demand that for those they loved. Even more astonishingly, they *did* seem to love her. Why? Because she could fight a little? As far as Lucious could see, any fool could do that. Many fools did. If the people had any sense, they would give their love where it was deserved: to their rightful rulers.

"I understand that she cannot simply be executed, your majesty," Stephania said, with one of those innocent smiles that Lucious had noticed she did so well.

"I'm glad you understand it," the king said, with obvious annoyance. "Do you also understand what would happen if she

21

were harmed now? Now that she has fought? Now that she has won?"

Of course Lucious understood. He wasn't some child for whom politics was an alien landscape.

Stephania summed it up. "It would fuel the revolution, your majesty. The people of the city might revolt."

"There is no 'might' about it," King Claudius said. "We have the Stade for a reason. The people have a thirst for blood, and we give them what they are looking for. That need for violence can turn against us just as easily."

Lucious laughed at that. It was hard to believe that the king really thought Delos's populace would ever be able to sweep them away. He had seen them, and they were not some blood-drenched tide. They were a rabble. Teach them a lesson, he thought. Kill enough of them, show them the consequences of their actions harshly enough, and they would soon fall into line.

"Is something funny, Lucious?" the queen asked him, and Lucious could hear the sharp edge there. The king and queen did not like being laughed at. Thankfully, though, he had an answer.

"It is just that the answer to all of this seems obvious," Lucious said. "I am not asking for Ceres to be executed. I am saying that we underestimated her abilities as a fighter. Next time, we must not."

"And give her an excuse to become more popular if she wins?" Stephania asked. "She has become beloved by the people because of her victory."

Lucious smiled at that. "Have you seen the way the commoners react in the Stade?" he asked. He understood this part, even if the others did not.

He saw Stephania sniff. "I try not to watch them, cousin."

"But you will have heard them. They call the names of their favorites. They bay for blood. And when their favorites fall, what then?" He looked around, half expecting someone to have an answer for him. To his disappointment, no one did. Perhaps Stephania wasn't bright enough to see it. Lucious didn't mind that.

"They call the names of the new winners," Lucious explained. "They love them just as much as they loved the last ones. Oh, they call for this girl now, but when she lies bleeding on the sand, they will bay for her death as quickly as for anyone else. We just have to stack the odds a little more against her."

The king looked thoughtful at that. "What did you have in mind?"

"If we get this wrong," the queen said, "they will just love her more."

Finally, Lucious could feel some of his anger being replaced by something else: satisfaction. He looked over to the doors to the throne room, where one of his attendants was standing waiting. A snap of his fingers was all it took to send the man running, but then, all Lucious's servants quickly learned that angering him was anything but wise.

"I have a remedy for that," Lucious said, gesturing toward the door.

The shackled man who walked in was easily more than seven feet tall, with ebony black skin and muscles that bulged above the short kilt he wore. Tattoos covered his flesh; the slaver who had sold the combatlord had told Lucious that each one represented a foe he had slain in single combat, both within the Empire and in the lands far to the south where he had been found.

Even so, for Lucious, the most intimidating part of it all wasn't the size of the man or his strength. It was the look in his eyes. There was something there that simply didn't seem to understand things like compassion or mercy, pain or fear. That could happily have torn them all limb from limb without feeling a thing. There were scars on the warrior's torso where blades had struck him. Lucious couldn't imagine that expression changing even then.

Lucious enjoyed watching the reactions of the others there as they saw the fighter, chained like some wild beast and stalking through them. Some of the women made small sounds of fear, while the men stepped back hurriedly out of his path, seeming to sense instinctively just how dangerous this man was. Fear seemed to push emptiness ahead of him, and Lucious basked in the effect his combatlord had. He watched Stephania take a scurrying step back out of the way, and Lucious smiled.

"They call him the Last Breath," Lucious said. "He has never lost a bout, and never let a foe live. Say hello," he grinned, "to Ceres's next—and final—opponent."

CHAPTER SIX

Ceres woke to darkness, the room lit only by moonlight filtering in through the shutters, and by a single flickering candle. She struggled toward consciousness, remembering. She remembered the beast's claws ripping at her, and just the memory seemed to be enough to summon the pain to her. It flared in her back as she half turned to her side, hot and sudden enough to make her cry out. The pain was all-consuming.

"Oh," a voice said, "does it hurt?"

A figure stepped into view. Ceres couldn't make out the details at first, but slowly, they swam into place. Stephania stood there over her bed, as pale as the shafts of moonlight that surrounded her, forming a perfect picture of the innocent noble, there to visit the sick and injured. Ceres had no doubt that it was deliberate.

"Don't worry," Stephania said. To Ceres, the words still seemed to come from too far away, fighting their way through fog. "The healers here gave you something to help you sleep while they stitched you back together. They seemed quite impressed you're still alive, and they wanted to take away your pain."

Ceres saw her hold up a small bottle. It was a dull green against the paleness of Stephania's hand, stoppered with a cork and glistening around the rim. Ceres saw the noble girl smile, and that smile felt as though it was made of sharp edges.

"*I* am not impressed that you have managed to live," Stephania said. "That wasn't the idea at *all.*"

Ceres tried to reach out for her. In theory, this should have been the moment to escape. If she had been stronger, she could have burst past Stephania and made for the door. If she could have found a way to fight past the cloudiness that felt as though it was filling her head to the breaking point, she might have been able to grab Stephania and force her to help in escaping.

Yet it seemed as if her body was only obeying her sluggishly, responding long after she wanted it to. It was all Ceres could do to sit up with the covers wrapped around her, and even that brought with it a fresh wave of agony.

She saw Stephania run a finger down the bottle she held. "Oh, don't worry, Ceres. There's a reason you're feeling so helpless. The healers asked me to make sure you got your dose of their drug, so I did. Some of it, anyway. Enough to keep you docile. Not enough to actually take away your pain."

"What did I do to make you hate me this much?" Ceres asked, although she already knew the answer. She'd been close to Thanos, and he'd rejected Stephania. "Does having Thanos for your husband really matter to you this much?"

"You're slurring your words, Ceres," Stephania said, with another of those smiles without any warmth behind it that Ceres could see. "And I don't hate you. Hate would imply that you were in some way worthy of being my enemy. Tell me, do you know anything about poison?"

Just the mention of it was enough to make Ceres's heart speed up, anxiety blossoming in her chest.

"Poison is such an elegant weapon," Stephania said, as though Ceres weren't even there. "Far more so than knives or spears. You think you are so strong because you get to play with swords with all the real combatlords? Yet I could have poisoned you while you slept, so easily. I could have added something to your sleeping draught. I could simply have given you too much of it, so that you never woke up."

"People would have known," Ceres managed.

Stephania shrugged. "Would they have cared? In any case, it would have been an accident. Poor Stephania, trying to help, but not really knowing what she was doing, gave our newest combatlord too much medicine."

She put a hand to her mouth in mock surprise. It was such a perfect mime of shocked remorse, even down to the tear that seemed to glisten at the corner of her eye. When she spoke again, she sounded different to Ceres. Her voice was thick with regret and disbelief. There was even a small catch there, as if she were struggling to hold back the urge to sob.

"Oh no. What have I done? I didn't mean to. I thought… I thought I did everything exactly the way they told me to!"

She laughed then, and in that moment, Ceres saw her for what she was. She could see through the act that Stephania so carefully maintained all the time. How did no one notice? Ceres wondered. How could they not see what lay behind the beautiful smiles and the delicate laughter?

"They all think I'm stupid, you know," Stephania said. She stood straighter now, looking a lot more dangerous to Ceres than she had. "I take great care to *ensure* that they think I'm stupid. Oh, don't look so worried, I'm not going to poison you."

"Why not?" Ceres asked. She knew there had to be a reason.

She saw Stephania's expression harden in the candlelight, a frown creasing the otherwise smooth skin of her brow.

"Because that would be too easy," Stephania said. "After the way you and Thanos humiliated me, I would rather see you suffer. You both deserve it."

"There's nothing else you can do to me," Ceres said, although in that moment, it didn't feel like it. Stephania could have walked over to the bed and hurt her a hundred different ways, and Ceres knew she would have been powerless to stop it. Ceres knew the noble would have no idea how to fight, but she could have bested Ceres easily right then.

"Of course there is," Stephania said. "There are weapons in the world even better than poison. The right words, for instance. Let's see now. Which of these will hurt most? Your beloved Rexus is dead, of course. Let's start with that."

Ceres tried not to let any of the shock she felt show on her face. She tried not to let the grief rise up enough that the noble girl could see it. Yet she knew from the look of satisfaction on Stephania's face that there must have been some flicker.

"He died fighting for you," Stephania said. "I thought you would want to know that part. It does make it so much more… romantic."

"You're lying," Ceres insisted, but somewhere inside she knew that Stephania wouldn't be. She would only say something like this if it was a truth Ceres could check, something that would hurt and go on hurting as she found out the reality of it.

"I don't need to lie. Not when the truth is so much better," Stephania said. "Thanos is dead too. He died in the fighting for Haylon, right there on the beaches."

A fresh wave of grief hit Ceres, sweeping over her and threatening to wash away all sense of herself. She'd fought with Thanos before he'd left, about the death of her brother, and about what he was planning to do, fighting the rebellion. She had never thought they could be the last words she would say to him. She'd left a message with Cosmas specifically so that they wouldn't be.

"There's one more," Stephania said. "Your younger brother? Sartes? He has been taken for the army. I made sure that the draft takers didn't overlook him just because he was the brother of Thanos's weapon keeper."

Ceres did try to lunge at her this time, the anger that filled her fueling her leap for the noble girl. As weak as she was, though, there was no chance of success. She felt her legs tangling in the bed sheets, sending her tumbling to the floor, looking up at Stephania.

"How long do you think your brother will last in the army?" Stephania asked. Ceres saw her expression turn into something like a mockery of pity. "The poor boy. They are so cruel to the conscripts. They're all practically traitors, after all."

"Why?" Ceres managed.

Stephania spread her hands. "You took Thanos from me, and that was everything I had planned for my future. Now, I'm going to take everything from you."

"I'll kill you," Ceres promised.

Stephania laughed. "You won't have a chance. This"—she reached down to touch Ceres's back, and Ceres had to bite her lip to keep from screaming—"is nothing. That little fight in the Stade was nothing. The worst fights imaginable will be there waiting for you, again and again, until you die."

"You think people won't notice?" Ceres said. "You think they won't guess what you're doing? You threw me in there because you thought they'd rise up. What will they do if they think you're cheating them?"

She saw Stephania shake her head.

"People see what they want to see. With you, it seems as though they want to see their princess combatlord, the girl who can fight as well as any man. They'll believe it, and they'll love you, right up to the point where you're turned into a laughing stock out on the sands. They'll watch you torn to shreds, but before that, they'll cheer for it to happen."

Ceres could only watch as Stephania started for the door. The noble girl stopped, turning back toward her, and for a moment, she looked as sweet and innocent as ever.

"Oh, I almost forgot. I tried to give you your medicine, but I didn't think you'd knock it from my hand before I could give you enough."

She took out the vial she'd had before, and Ceres watched it tumble to the ground as she dropped it. It shattered, the pieces spinning across the floor of Ceres's room in splinters that would make it both painful and dangerous for her to try to find her way back into her bed. Ceres had no doubt that Stephania intended it that way.

She saw the noble girl reach out for the candle that lit the room, and briefly, in the instant before she snuffed it out, Stephania's sweet smile faded again, to be replaced by something cruel.

"I will be there to dance at your funeral, Ceres. I promise you that."

CHAPTER SEVEN

"I still say that we should gut him and throw his body out for the other Empire soldiers to find."

"That's because you're an idiot, Nico. Even if they noticed one more body among the rest, who's to say they'd care? And then we'd have the trouble of bringing him down somewhere they'd see him. No. We should ransom him."

Thanos sat in the cave where the rebels had holed up for the moment, listening to them argue about his fate. His hands were tied in front of him, but at least they'd done their best to patch and bandage his wounds, leaving him in front of a small fire so he wouldn't freeze while they decided whether to kill him in cold blood or not.

The rebels sat at other fires, huddling around them, discussing what they could do to keep the island from falling to the Empire. They spoke quietly, so that Thanos couldn't overhear the details, but he already knew the gist of it: they were losing, and losing badly. They were in the caves because there was nowhere else for them to go.

After a while, the one who was obviously their leader came and sat down opposite Thanos, crossing his legs on the hard stone of the cave floor. He pushed across a hunk of bread that Thanos devoured hungrily. He wasn't sure how long it had been since he'd last eaten.

"I am Akila," the other man said. "I command this rebellion."

"Thanos."

"Just Thanos?"

Thanos could hear the curiosity there, and the impatience. He wondered if the other man had guessed who he was. Either way, the truth seemed like the best option right then.

"Prince Thanos," he admitted.

Akila sat there opposite him for several seconds, and Thanos found himself wondering if he was going to die then. It had been close enough when the rebels had thought he was just some noble without a name. Now that they knew he was one of the royal family, close to the king who had oppressed them so much, it seemed impossible that they would do anything else.

"A prince," Akila said. He looked around at the others, and Thanos saw the flash of a smile there. "Hey, lads, we've got ourselves a prince here."

"We should definitely ransom him then!" one of the rebels called out. "He'd be worth a fortune!"

"We should definitely kill him," another snapped back. "Think about all his kind have done to us!"

"All right, that's enough," Akila said. "Concentrate on the fight ahead. It's going to be a long night."

Thanos heard a faint sigh from the other man as the men went back to their fires.

"It's not going well, then?" Thanos said. "You said before that your side was losing."

Akila gave him a sharp look. "I should know when to keep my mouth shut. Maybe so should you."

"You're wondering whether to kill me anyway," Thanos pointed out. "I figure that I don't have a lot to lose."

Thanos waited. This wasn't the kind of man he could push into giving him answers. There was something tough about Akila. Unyielding and straightforward. Thanos guessed that he would have liked him if they'd met under better circumstances.

"All right," Akila said. "Yes, we're losing. You Imperials have more men than we do, and you don't care about the damage you do. The city is under siege from land and from water, so that no one can get away. We'll fight from the hills, but when you can just resupply by water, there's not a lot we can do. Draco may be a butcher, but he's a clever one."

Thanos nodded. "He is."

"And of course, you were probably there when he planned all of it," Akila said.

Now Thanos understood. "Is that what you're hoping? That I know all of their plans?" He shook his head. "I wasn't there when they made them. I didn't want to be here, and I only came because they escorted me onto the ship under guard. Maybe if I had been there, I would have heard the part where they planned to stab me in the back."

He thought of Ceres then, about the way he'd been forced to leave her behind. That hurt more than the rest of it put together. If someone in a position of power was going to try to have him killed, he wondered, what would they do to her?

"You have enemies," Akila agreed. Thanos saw him clench and unclench one hand, as if the long battle for the city had started to make it cramp. "They're even the same as my enemies. I don't know if that makes you my friend, though."

Thanos looked around pointedly at the rest of the cave. At the shockingly low numbers of soldiers left there. "Right now, it looks as though you could do with all the friends you can get."

"You're still a noble. You still have your position because of the blood of ordinary folk," Akila said. He sighed again. "It looks as though if I kill you, I'm doing what Draco and his masters want, but you've as good as told me that if I ransom you, I get nothing for you. I have a fight to win, and no time to keep prisoners around if they don't know anything. So, what am I supposed to do with you, Prince Thanos?"

Thanos got the impression that he was serious. That he actually wanted a better solution. Thanos thought quickly.

"I think your best choice is to let me go," he said.

Akila laughed at that. "Nice try. If that's the best you have, hold still. I'll try to make this as painless as possible."

Thanos saw his hand go to one of his swords.

"I'm serious," Thanos said. "I can't help you win the battle for the island if I'm here."

He could see Akila's disbelief, and the certainty that it had to be a trap. Thanos went on quickly, knowing that his best hope of surviving the next few minutes lay in convincing this man that he wanted to help the rebellion.

"You said yourself that one of the big problems is that the Empire has its fleet supporting the assault," Thanos said. "I know that they left supplies on the ships because they were so eager to get on with the attack. So we take the ships."

Akila stood up. "Have you heard this, lads? The prince here has a plan to take the Empire's ships from them."

Thanos saw the rebels start to gather round.

"What good would it do?" Akila asked. "We take their ships, but what then?"

Thanos did his best to explain. "At the very least, it will provide an escape route for some of the people of the city, and for more of your soldiers. It will take away supplies from the Empire's soldiers too, so that they can't keep going for long. And then there are the ballistae."

"What are they?" one of the rebels called out. He didn't look much like a long-term soldier. Very few of those in the room did, to Thanos's eyes.

"Bolt throwers," Thanos explained. "Weapons designed to damage other ships, but if they were turned against soldiers near the shore…"

Akila, at least, looked as though he was considering the possibilities. "That could be something," he admitted. "And we can set light to any ships we can't use. At the very least, Draco would pull his men back to try to get his ships back. But how do we get

30

these ships in the first place, Prince Thanos? I know that where you come from, if a prince asks for something, he gets it, but I doubt that will apply to Draco's fleet."

Thanos forced himself to smile with a level of confidence he didn't feel. "That's almost exactly what we're going to do."

Again, Thanos had the impression of Akila working it out faster than any of his men could. The rebel leader smiled.

"You're mad," Akila said. Thanos couldn't tell if it was intended as an insult or not.

"There are enough dead on the beaches," Thanos explained, for the benefit of the others. "We take their armor and head to the ships. With me there, it will look like a company of soldiers returning from the battle for supplies."

"What do you think?" Akila asked.

In the firelight that flickered inside the cave, Thanos couldn't make out the men who spoke. Instead, their questions seemed to emerge from the darkness, so that he couldn't tell who agreed with him, who doubted him, and who wanted him dead. Still, it was no worse than the politics back home. Better, in a lot of ways, since at least no one was smiling to his face while plotting to kill him.

"What about guards on the ships?" one of the rebels asked.

"There won't be many," Thanos said. "And they'll know who I am."

"What about all the people who will die in the city while we do this?" another called out.

"They're dying now," Thanos insisted. "At least this way, you have a way to fight back. Get this right, and we'll have a way to save hundreds, if not thousands, of them."

Silence fell, and the last question came out of it like an arrow.

"How can we trust him, Akila? He's not just one of them, he's a *noble*. A *prince*."

Thanos whirled away from the direction the voice had come from, offering up his back for anyone to see. "They stabbed me in the back. They left me to die. I have as much reason to hate them as any man here."

In that moment, he wasn't just thinking about the Typhoon. He was thinking about everything his family had done to the people of Delos, and about everything they'd done to Ceres. If they hadn't forced him to go to Fountain Square, he would never have been there when her brother died.

"We could sit here," Thanos said, "or we could act. Yes, it will be dangerous. If they see through our disguise, we're probably

31

dead. I'm willing to risk it. Are you?" When no one answered, Thanos raised his voice. "*Are you?*"

That got a cheer in response. Akila stepped close to him, clapping a hand on Thanos's shoulder.

"All right, Prince, it looks like we're doing things your way. Pull this off, and you'll have a friend for life." His hand tightened until Thanos could feel pain shooting through his back. "Betray us, though, get my men killed, and I swear I'll hunt you down."

CHAPTER EIGHT

There were parts of Delos where Berin didn't normally go. They were parts that stank to him of sweat and desperation, as people did whatever they needed to in order to get by. He waved away offers from the shadows, giving the denizens there hard looks to keep them back.

If they'd known about the gold he carried, Berin knew he would have found himself with his throat cut, the purse beneath his tunic divided up and spent in the local taverns and gambling houses before the day was done. It was those places he sought out now, because where else was he going to find soldiers when they were off duty? As a bladesmith, Berin knew fighting men, and he knew the places they would go.

He had gold because he'd visited a merchant, taking with him two daggers he'd forged as examples for those who might have employed him. They'd been beautiful things, worthy of any noble's belt, worked with gold filigree and etched with hunting scenes on the blades. They were the last things of value he had left in the world. He'd stood in line with a dozen other people in front of the merchant's desk, and hadn't gotten half of what he knew they were worth.

To Berin, that didn't matter. All that mattered was finding his children, and that took gold. Gold he could use to buy ale for the right people, gold he could press into the right palms.

He made his way through Delos's taverns, and it was a slow process. He couldn't just come out and ask the questions he wanted to ask. He had to be careful. It helped that he had a few friends in the city, and a few more in the Empire's army. His blades had saved more than a few men's lives, over the years.

He found the man he was looking for half drunk in the middle of the afternoon, sitting in a tavern and stinking so much that he had clear space all around him. Berin guessed that it was only the uniform of the Empire's army that kept them from throwing him face first into the street. Well, that and the fact that Jacare was fat enough that it would have taken half the inn's patrons to lift him.

Berin saw the fat man's eyes lift up as he approached. "Berin? My old friend! Come and have a drink with me! Although you'll have to pay. I'm currently a little…"

"Fat? Drunk?" Berin guessed. He knew the other man wouldn't mind. The soldier seemed to make an effort to be the Imperial army's worst example. He even seemed to take a perverse kind of pride in it.

"...financially embarrassed," Jacare finished.

"I might be able to help with that," Berin said. He ordered drinks, but didn't touch his. He needed to keep a clear head if he was going to find Ceres and Sartes. Instead, he waited while Jacare downed his with a noise that sounded to Berin like a donkey at a water trough.

"So, what brings a man like you to my humble presence?" Jacare asked after a while.

"I'm looking for news," Berin said. "The kind of news a man in your position might have heard."

"Ah, well, *news*. News is a thirsty business. And possibly an expensive one."

"I'm looking for my son and daughter," Berin explained. With someone else, it might have gained him some sympathy, but he knew that with a man like this, it wouldn't have much effect.

"Your son? Nesos, right?"

Berin leaned across the table, his hand closing over Jacare's wrist as the man went to take another drink. He didn't have much of the old strength left that he'd built wielding forge hammers, but there was still enough to make the other man wince. Good, Berin thought.

"Sartes," Berin said. "My eldest son is dead. Sartes has been taken by the army. I know you hear things. I want to know where he is, and I want to know where my daughter, Ceres, is."

Jacare sat back, and Berin let him do it. He wasn't sure he could have held the other man in place much longer anyway.

"That's the kind of thing I might have heard," the soldier admitted, "but that kind of thing is difficult. I have expenses."

Berin brought out the small pouch of gold. He poured it out onto the table, just far enough from the other man that Jacare couldn't snatch it easily.

"Will this cover your 'expenses'?" Berin asked, with a look at the other man's drinking goblet. He saw the other man counting the gold, probably gauging whether there was any more to be had.

"Your daughter is the easy one," Jacare said. "She's up at the castle with the nobles. They announced that she was to marry Prince Thanos."

Berin dared to breathe a sigh of relief at that, even though he wasn't sure what to think. Thanos was one of the few royals with any decency to him, but marriage?

"Your son is trickier. Let me think. I heard that a few of the recruiters from the Twenty-third were doing the rounds down by your quarter, but there's no guarantee that it's them. If it is, they're camped a little way to the south, trying to train up the conscripts to fight rebels."

Bile rose in Berin's mouth at that thought. He could guess how the army would treat Sartes, and just what that "training" would involve. He had to get his son back. But Ceres was closer, and the truth was that he had to at least see his daughter before he went after Sartes. He stood.

"Not going to finish your drink?" Jacare asked.

Berin didn't answer. He was going to the castle.

***

It was easier for Berin to get into the castle than it would have been for almost anyone else. It had been a while, but he was still the one who had come there to discuss the requirements for combatlords' weapons, or to bring special pieces for the nobles. It was simple enough to pretend that he was back in business, heading straight past the guards on the outer gates and into the space where the fighters prepared.

The next step was to get from there to wherever his daughter was. There was a barred gateway between the vaulted space where the warriors practiced and the rest of the castle. Berin had to wait for that to open from the other side, pushing past the servant who did it and trying to pretend that he had important business elsewhere in the building.

He did, just not the kind that most of the people there would understand.

"Hey, you! Where do you think you're going?"

Berin froze at the rough tone of that. He knew before he turned that there would be a guard there, and he didn't have an excuse that would satisfy them. The best he could hope for now would be to be thrown out of the castle before he could get close to seeing his daughter. The worst would involve the castle's dungeons, or maybe just being dragged away to be executed where no one would ever know.

He turned and saw two guards who had obviously been soldiers of the Empire for a while. They had as much gray in their hair as Berin did these days, with the weathered look of men who'd spent too much time fighting in the sun over too many years. One was a good head taller than Berin, but stooped slightly over the spear he leaned on. The other had a beard that he'd oiled and waxed until it looked almost as sharp as the weapon he held. Relief flooded through Berin as he saw them, because he recognized them both.

"Varo, Caxus?" Berin said. "It's me, Berin."

The tension hung there for a moment, and Berin found himself hoping that the two would remember him. Then the guards laughed.

"So it is," Varo said, unbending from over his spear for a moment. "We haven't seen you in... how long has it been, Caxus?"

The other stroked his beard while he considered. "It's been months since he was last here. Haven't really talked since he delivered those bracers for me last summer."

"I've been away," Berin explained. He didn't say where. People might not pay their smiths much, but he doubted they would react well to him looking for work elsewhere. Soldiers didn't usually like the idea of their enemies receiving good blades. "Times have been hard."

"Times have been hard all around," Caxus agreed. Berin saw him frown slightly. "It still doesn't explain what you're doing in the main castle."

"You shouldn't be in here, bladesmith, and you know it," Varo agreed.

"What is it?" Caxus asked. "An emergency repair for some noble lad's favorite sword? I think we'd have heard if Lucious had snapped a blade. He'd probably have flogged his servants raw."

Berin knew he wouldn't be able to get away with a lie like that. Instead, he decided to try the one thing that might work: honesty. "I'm here to see my daughter."

He heard Varo suck in air between his teeth. "Ah, now that's a tricky one."

Caxus nodded. "Saw her fighting in the Stade the other day. Tough little thing. She killed a spiny bear and a combatlord. Hard fight though."

Berin's heart tightened in his chest as he heard that. They had Ceres fighting on the sands? Even though he knew it had been her dream to fight there, this didn't feel like the fulfillment of it. No, this was something else.

"I have to see her," Berin insisted.

Varo tilted his head to one side. "Like I said, tricky. No one gets in to see her now. Queen's orders."

"But I'm her father," Berin said.

Caxus spread his hands. "There's not a lot we can do."

Berin thought quickly. "Not a lot you can do? Was that what I said when you needed your spear re-hafting before your captain saw that you'd snapped it that time?"

"We said we wouldn't talk about that," the guard said, with a worried look.

"And what about you, Varo?" Berin continued, pressing his point home before the other could decide to throw him out. "Did I say that it was 'tricky' when you wanted a sword that would actually fit your hand, rather than army issue?"

"Well..."

Berin didn't stop. The important thing was to push forward past their objections. No, the *important* thing was to see his daughter.

"How many times has my work saved your lives?" he demanded. "Varo, you told me the story of that bandit chief your unit went after. Whose sword did you use to kill him?"

"Yours," Varo admitted.

"And Caxus, when you wanted all that filigree work on your greaves to impress that girl you married, who did you go to?"

"You," Caxus said. Berin could see him pondering.

"And that's before we get to the days when I was following you all around on campaign," Berin said. "What about—"

Caxus raised a hand. "All right, all right. You've made your point. Your daughter's room is further up. We'll show you the way. But if anyone asks, we're just escorting you *out* of the building."

Berin doubted anyone would ask, but that didn't matter right then. Only one thing did. He was going to see his daughter. He followed the two along the castle's corridors, finally coming to a door that was barred and locked from the outside. Since the key sat in the lock, he turned it.

Berin's heart nearly burst at his first sight of his daughter for months. She lay in bed, groaning as she came to, and looking at him with bleary eyes.

"Father?"

"Ceres!" Berin ran to her, throwing his arms around her and crushing her tight to him. "It's okay. I'm here."

He wanted to hold her tightly and never let her go right then, but he heard Ceres's gasp of pain as he hugged her, and he pulled back hurriedly.

"What's wrong?" Berin asked.

"No, it's all right," Ceres said. "I'm fine."

"You're not fine," Berin said. His daughter had always been so strong, so if she was in pain, it had to be bad. Berin never wanted to see his daughter hurt like that. "Let me look."

Ceres let him, and Berin winced at what he saw. Tightly stitched wounds ran in parallel lines across his daughter's back.

"How did you get in here?" Ceres asked while he did it. "How did you even find me?"

"I still have some friends," her father said. "And I wasn't going to give up without finding you."

Ceres turned to him, and Berin could see the love there in her eyes. "I'm glad you're here."

"So am I," Berin said. "I should never have left you with your mother."

Ceres reached out to take his hand, and Berin had forgotten quite how much he missed his daughter until then. "You're here now."

"I am," Berin said. He took another look at her back. "They haven't cleaned it properly. Here, let me find something to help."

It was hard having to leave even for that short time. Varo and Caxus were still outside, and it didn't take much to get them to bring food and water. Maybe they saw the look on his face when it came to things that involved Ceres's well-being.

He passed her the bowl of food, and the speed with which Ceres devoured it told Berin everything he needed to know about how they'd been treating her here. He took the bowl of water, using it to clean out the wounds she'd gotten from her fight.

Ceres nodded. "I'm a lot better than I was."

"Then I don't want to think about how bad it was," Berin said.

He couldn't keep the guilt from washing up over him. If he hadn't gone, then his children would never have gone through any of this.

"I'm sorry, I should have been here."

"It might not have changed anything," Ceres said, and Berin could tell that she was trying to reassure him. "The rebellion would still have happened. I might still have fought in the Stade."

"Maybe." Berin didn't want to believe it. He knew Ceres had always had an attraction to the danger of the Stade, but that didn't mean she would have fought there. She might have been safe. "I could have protected you and your brothers."

Ceres took his hand again. "I think there are some things even you can't protect us from."

Berin smiled. "Do you remember when you were little? You used to think I was the strongest man in the world, and I could protect you from anything?"

Ceres smiled back. "Now I have to protect myself, and I'm strong enough to do it."

There was a part of Berin that was happy it was true, but he still wanted to be there for his daughter. "Either way, it's over. We'll get you out of here."

Berin thought about the guards. Exactly how much did they owe him? Exactly how much would they help before they decided it was easier to take him into custody?

"I'll find a way," Berin promised.

Ceres shook her head quickly. "No. I'm not running away."

"I know you're worried about being caught," Berin said, covering her hand with his, "but I think I have enough friends in the castle to get us both out. We could join the rebellion."

"It's not about that," Ceres said. "This is my path. I'm here to fight. I'm meant to fight."

He stared back, stunned.

"You *want* to stay here?" That was hard to believe, especially when it had taken so much to find her. It had felt obvious that if he could only get inside, he could have his family back. "I thought you'd want to go. That we could find Sartes together, and everything would be all right."

"Everything will be all right," Ceres promised him. "And you should go to find Sartes. Get him safe."

She stood and dressed in her training clothes. For a moment, Berin thought that she might come with him after all, but she showed no sign of doing so.

"What are you doing?" he asked. "If you're not coming with me, you should rest."

"I can't," Ceres said. She turned back toward him, determination set on her face. "I'm going to train. They want to kill me, but I'm not going to let them. I'm not going to give up, and I'm not going to give them the satisfaction of seeing me run away."

Berin swallowed at the strength there in his daughter. Even so, he didn't want to just leave her. "I could come with you. I could help you."

Ceres shook her head.

"It is a path for me alone, Father."

He smiled at her, and he could feel his eyes well with tears, as he saw hers well, too. He had never been more proud of her, or loved her more.

He stepped forward as she did, and they embraced for a long time.

"I love you, Ceres," he whispered, "and I always will."

"I know, Father," she replied. "And whether we ever meet again or not, you should know that I love you, too."

CHAPTER NINE

Ceres focused, dodging, weaving, gasping for breath, bruises rising from where the sticks had struck her. Master Isel faced her in the training grounds, and she stared back. As she stood there, she wondered if she had been right to request that he train her again so soon. He had seemed doubtful she was well enough, barely recovered as she was from her injuries. Yet she had insisted, determined to get back out there, to better herself, to be ready for the next match.

To go down in the Stade fighting.

The moment she'd said that she was, Isel had taken Ceres at her word, and had pushed her harder than he'd ever pushed her before. He, too, seemed to know what was at stake.

"Move!" he cried.

Ceres tried to keep up with Master Isel's instructions as she whirled on the sparring grounds. He was using a pair of long sticks against her, swinging them so that Ceres had to dodge and parry with the practice blade she held.

"Circle the other way!" he bellowed, as Ceres took a step to her right. She had to dodge back as he thrust with one of the sticks. "Don't go straight back. Do you want an enemy to chase you down? No, no, not like that!"

One of the sticks swept round, knocking Ceres's sword from her hand as it smashed into her forearm. She felt a stab of pain and watched as it landed point-first in the sand.

"Extend your sword when you are not attacking, and you will lose the arm!"

Master Isel swung around his sticks at Ceres's head to demonstrate his point. Ceres threw herself into a roll, coming up with her sword in her hand.

Ceres leaped and dodged, blocked and avoided. Even so, some of the blows got through. One knocked the air from her lungs, and she had to force herself to keep fighting. She fought until she could barely see, sweat stinging her eyes.

Finally, Isel stepped back, studying her, signaling it was time to rest.

She leaned on her sword and took a break.

Out of the corner of her eye Ceres glimpsed Lucious stepping down onto the sands to train. He strode in wearing full armor, though no one else there wore any. He looked about him, gestured to a weapon keeper, and started to spar with him, even though the weapon keeper clearly had no experience. Lucious seemed to be delighting in slamming his practice blade into his unprotected opponent.

Ceres stopped to watch when suddenly a sharp blow from one of Master Isel's sticks snapped her out of it.

"It was time to rest!" she exclaimed, indignant.

He smiled.

"Never trust your opponent."

Ceres began her dance with the constantly moving sticks again. On and on it went, until finally, Master Isel stepped back.

"That will do for now," he said with a nod. "Get water, then we go again."

Ceres walked over to where a group of the other fighters were standing around a water barrel, drinking water out of it using a ladle. Ceres was expecting to have to edge round them or wait until they were done. Instead, a combatlord with tightly corded muscles and shaved hair passed across the ladle.

"You did well," he said. "The first time Master Isel used the sticks with me, I got knocked flat a dozen times."

A shorter combatlord with thinning hair nodded. When he spoke, it was obvious to Ceres that he'd come to the Empire from the northerners' lands. "Did well with your fight too. Didn't run. A beast like that, most people back off, but you went in. Good instincts."

The others didn't speak, but they didn't need to. It was enough for Ceres that they seemed to accept her there, making room for her among them as she got the refreshment she needed.

Of course, Lucious had to be the one to spoil it for her. He pushed toward the water butt, as if he couldn't have sent a dozen servants running for refreshments.

"Out of my way, peasants," he snapped at the combatlords. Ceres thought she saw one of them smile.

"Thought I heard something," he said.

Another shrugged. "Probably just the wind."

Lucious stepped round them, and now Ceres could see his face reddening. He stood before her, and Ceres suspected that if they'd been alone he would have struck her. It was probably as well that they weren't, she decided. She would only have gotten in trouble again for striking him back.

"You think you're clever?" he asked her. "You think that you're some kind of real warrior because you survived one fight in the Stade?"

"I'm not the one who ran from the arena," she said.

41

That only seemed to make Lucious turn redder. He reached for his belt, where a sword sat. No, not just any sword. As he drew it, Ceres saw that it was the sword her father had made for her. She wanted to reach out and grab it in that moment, because no one like Lucious should ever get to touch something her father had made.

"Recognize this?" Lucious said. Then he did something Ceres would have thought was unthinkable: he started to strip the blade down, taking it apart to its component parts. He unwound the leather of the handle, pulling off the gold wire. He unfastened the pommel, pulling the guard free of the tang. "I'm a little bored of it."

Ceres had to swallow her own anger. She felt the hand of one of the combatlords on her shoulder, holding her back or offering support, she wasn't sure which. How could Lucious do something like that? Didn't he know how much work went into a sword like that? Scraps of metal fell to the ground, but Lucious didn't seem to care.

"Forgive me, my lord," Master Isel said, approaching. "But I think these lay-abouts have had enough of a break. Back to work with you, all of you."

Ceres wanted to ignore the instruction. She wanted to punch the smile right off Lucious's face, but she went back to the sands as Master Isel instructed.

Lucious called out to her as she went. "Train as much as you want. It won't work. Tomorrow you'll face *my* man in the Stade, and all the dancing around with sticks in the world won't save you!"

CHAPTER TEN

Thanos should have been used to marching at the head of units of men, leading them into battle. He was a noble, trained in violence, and had fought in the Stade.

He'd never been in a position quite like this, though.

The band at his back looked like Empire soldiers. At least, they looked as close to Empire soldiers as they'd been able to manage while taking uniforms and armor from the dead. Yet it was easy for Thanos to see that there wasn't the same rigid discipline among them, maintained by the threat of the lash or the executioner's blade. The rebels didn't quite keep step with him as they marched, and they carried their own mixture of weapons, rather than anything officially issued by the army's quartermasters.

"This had better work," Akila said as they marched into view of the army's landing craft.

"It will work," Thanos promised him. He hoped that it was true. "Just… try not to kill anyone if you don't have to."

"Want us to go soft on your Empire friends?" Akila asked. Thanos could hear the suspicion there.

"I want you to remember that these are just ordinary men."

"Who chose to attack our island," Akila pointed out.

They marched down all the beach front, where the landing boats still sat, the rowing craft dragged up above the tide line. There were guards there with them now, who looked up sharply as they approached.

"Halt, who goes!" the nearest called.

"Can't you see?" Thanos called back. It was hard to make it sound natural. "I have troops who need to resupply on the main ships."

The solider offered a hurried bow. "Forgive me, your highness, I didn't know it was you. But these ships are meant to stay here. Orders."

"Orders from someone higher than your prince?" Akila demanded, beside Thanos. To Thanos's ears, he did a perfect impression of some toady drunk on reflected glory.

"No, of course, sir."

"Then get these boats into the water!"

The guards stood back. Some of them actually helped the rebels carry the landing craft out into the breakers.

"I can't believe we've done this," Thanos heard a one of the rebels say. He shook his head.

43

"This part is just the start," Thanos said. "We still need the main ships."

Akila's men set to the oars, pulling back from the beach with smooth strokes that took them in the direction of the ships further out. Those cut menacing profiles in the water, bolt throwers and fire slings in their prows adding to the sense of threat they emanated. The small boats spread out, each heading for a different ship.

"If those things fire on us," Akila pointed out, "they'll sink us before we get close."

Thanos tried to project confidence. "They won't fire."

The rebel leader didn't seem convinced, but he stayed silent as they approached the ships. Thanos guessed that he didn't want to risk his fears spreading to his men. Instead, he stood there in the prow, waiting like a figurehead until the ships stood towering above them.

"Who's down there?" a sailor asked, leaning over the side. "Do you need supplies?"

Obviously, the combination of the Empire's boats and the Empire's uniforms was enough. Even so Thanos could feel the tension in the moment. He could also see Akila reaching for a knife.

"It's Thanos," he said. "Let us aboard."

The sailor stepped back, and they clambered up the netting that hung from the side of the ship exactly for that purpose, climbing onto the deck in a way they never could have hoped to if they'd been trying to board by force. The sailors would have cut them to pieces as they appeared over the gunwale, or simply shoved them overboard to drown. There weren't many sailors aboard—Thanos guessed most would have gone ashore with the landing parties—but there would have been enough.

"Prince Thanos," one asked, "do you need medical attention? You look as though you've been bleeding."

Thanos stood on the deck, looking out over the bay near Haylon. From where he was, he could see the siege of the city's waterfront, with Empire soldiers there swarming against the walls. The defenders had obviously managed to seal the city for now, but there was nowhere for them to escape to, and the attackers had the weapons on the ships with which to attack the walls. Already, parts of the city were on fire.

"No," Thanos said. "That isn't what we need."

It felt bad to have to do what he did next. This man probably had a family somewhere, and was probably only there at all because he'd been made to. The only good part about this was that at least Thanos could make sure that he came through this alive.

He struck out, catching the man on the jaw as cleanly as he could, feeling the connection as his knuckles struck home. The sailor tumbled to the deck, and Akila's people piled forward.

A sailor ran at Thanos, an awl in his hand with the sharp point set to stab downwards. Thanos ducked, catching the arm and throwing the man over his hip. He came up on top, grabbing the arm that held the weapon with both hands. He could have reached for a blade of his own, but Thanos didn't want to kill if he could avoid it. These men weren't the ones to blame. It was the ones who ruled them who had started this. Instead, he brought his elbow down in a short arc that ended with his opponent unconscious.

He looked up to find that Akila's men had already taken the rest of the ship. On the ships nearby, Thanos could see violence breaking out, although with the rebels wearing Empire colors, it was almost impossible to see who was winning.

"Do you think we're succeeding?" Thanos asked.

Akila nodded. "My men are tough. They'll signal when they have the ships."

Sure enough, one by one, men on the other ships nearby started to wave their success. Only a few of the ships on the fringes were left untaken.

"So now what, Prince?" Akila asked. "We have some ships. What do we do with them?"

Thanos nodded to the ballista that sat on the forecastle of their ship. "Now, we do what we can to stop the siege."

He hated this part. He wished that there were another way, but unless they did this, the Empire's forces would soon overwhelm Haylon. Akila and his men made their way toward the siege weapon, loading it with a bolt as long as a man was tall. They set light to it, so that Thanos could see the flames flickering as they turned it toward one of the ships they hadn't been able to take. He thought he could see some of the sailors over there moving in sudden panic as they realized that things weren't as they should be.

By then, it was already too late. Akila gestured to the firing lever. "You got us this far, Prince. We wouldn't have gotten the boats without you. You should be the one to start this."

Thanos knew it was a test. Could he do this? He looked over at the ship, where the men were still struggling to do something about the danger, then over at the city, where the Empire's soldiers were ravaging their way along the waterfront. He couldn't pretend not to know what the weapons would do. He'd helped to come up with this plan knowing all of that. Part of Thanos insisted that this was wrong, and that he would be killing his own soldiers. How many men would die if he did this? he wondered.

How many would die if he didn't? Thanos had heard General Draco. There was to be no quarter for anyone who resisted. The army in front of him was there bent on pillage and destruction, so that soon, no one in the city would be safe. He had to do this.

Thanos felt the roughness of the wood as he wrapped his hand around the firing lever, then he pulled.

The first bolt sang through the air to catch in the sails of its target. The fire caught quickly, smoke coming up from the stricken ship in moments, and flames following. Sailors ran to put the flames out, but more bolts were already flying.

They struck at the ships they hadn't been able to take first, firing in volleys of flaming bolts and ceramic pots filled with tar. Many missed. Most missed, but Thanos saw enough strike home to matter, fire after fire starting on the enemy ships. He saw sailors running about, trying to stop the fires, or fire back, or get their ships to safety. He saw more and more dive into the relative safety of Haylon's waters, preferring to take their chances with the sharks that had come there for the dead rather than risk the fire.

They turned their attention toward the city then. Thanos guessed that the troops on the waterfront would have realized that something was badly wrong, but they still seemed to be intent upon their attack. It was only as bolts started to fall among them that they started to scatter.

"Three more volleys," Akila said. "Then we have to go. My men are already getting ready to fire the ships."

Thanos nodded. He wished they could keep the ships, but the truth was that they didn't have the men to hold them, or the skills to sail them. The best they could do was to deprive the Empire of its supplies.

He made his way to one of the men he'd knocked out, shaking the man until he came awake again. The sailor thrashed in his grip, trying to break free.

"We're going to burn this ship," he yelled, as the man struggled. "You have a choice. You can stay here to fight me, or you can take your chances swimming for shore."

It wasn't a choice that took the other man long to make. The sailor took one look at Thanos and dove for the side, the splash as he entered the water sending spray up high. Already, Thanos could see Akila and the rebels firing the last of their bolts at the soldiers on the shore, while others broke open the ceramic globes holding tar, spreading it over the deck. They set light to it, and instantly,

Thanos could feel the heat of the flames as they rose up to consume the ship.

"Everybody off!" Akila ordered. He clapped a hand on Thanos's shoulder. "That means you too, Prince."

Now, it didn't seem so much like an insult as it had. Thanos dropped over the side of the ship, pulling himself into the landing boat. Around him, Akila's men pressed their way into position. Thanos took an oar, hauling on it as they set the boat into motion over the waves. Behind them, the Empire's fleet was slowly turning into a bonfire.

Thanos saw him nod in the direction of the city.

"The bad news," Akila said, "is that even with their supplies gone, there's still more Empire soldiers than us. We've a lot of fighting ahead of us. Are you ready for that, Prince?"

Thanos looked out toward the waterfront, where soldiers were still attacking in scattered clumps. They were the army belonging to his land, his king. Right then, though, he had never felt more strongly that he was on the right side.

He nodded. "I'm ready."

"Well, Prince," Akila said with a smile, "looks like we're not going to be killing you after all."

CHAPTER ELEVEN

Ceres was sweating in the night air, and not from sparring, for once. Instead, she was stuck scrubbing the tiles of one of the castle's courtyards, wiping away the mud and dirt that had collected there. She had no doubt that this was Lucious's doing; just another way of him making life harder for her there, and maybe a way of wearing her down before her fight too.

Of course, she had to do her cleaning where she would have a good view of the castle's main hall, and where those within would be able to look out and laugh at her. There was a feast taking place in there, complete with dancing and lavish entertainments. Ceres could see Lucious, Stephania, and all the other royals enjoying themselves, eating delicate pastries and drinking wines that had probably been brought from all corners of the Empire. Girls in elaborate dresses danced with young men who strode around the place looking as though they'd decided they deserved all the attention in the world.

Seeing them there like that was difficult. Ceres scrubbed the tiles because she had no doubt that they'd take any excuse to punish her, but she didn't mind hard work. She'd done worse than this when her mother had set her endless chores back home. The hard part was seeing them enjoying themselves when she was stuck out here. It was the knowledge that she would never be good enough for any of them, no matter what she did.

Even if she had been there, Ceres knew, they would have treated her as nothing. She would have been just one more of the servants and slaves who moved through the hall, offering food and drink, dancing or singing for their amusement.

Thanos was the only one who treated her any differently, and now he was gone. Just the thought of that made Ceres stare up at the stars above, looking for answers among their pinpoints. How could he have died? Only the thought that Stephania might have lied to her kept Ceres going then, and the truth was that Stephania had no reason to lie. As she'd said, the truth was more painful.

Ceres sat watching the feast then. The queen sat daintily, drinking from a crystal goblet while around her, lesser nobles formed concentric rings of power and gossip. The king sat separately, at the head of the longest table, where some of the younger noblemen were already drunk enough to start making grabs for the serving girls. Just the sight of it all made Ceres sick.

I will win tomorrow, she told herself. *Whatever they throw at me*.

What would happen after that, though? Match after match in the Stade, with no time to recover from her injuries? Her back was healing well, but the physical work of scrubbing the tiles felt as though it was almost designed to open up the wounds again. How soon would there be an injury she couldn't recover from? Ceres couldn't imagine Stephania or Lucious holding back, no matter how bad things got.

Ceres could see Stephania there, dancing with Lucious. She moved with such delicate grace, like a jeweled butterfly flitting her way around him. If Lucious occasionally shot glances in the direction of the other young women there, Stephania appeared not to notice. It was hard for Ceres to guess exactly how much she saw. She certainly didn't seem to have been affected by the news of Thanos's death.

It will get worse, Ceres told herself. They will find a way to make it worse. She was certain of that much. It wasn't just about who she was now. It was about the symbol she'd become. The girl who could fight in the Stade and win. The commoner who could stand up to the power of the royals and live. She'd been the girl who was going to marry a prince, too, and Ceres knew that Stephania, at least, hated her as much for that as any of the rest of it.

They would find a way to make it worse for her. They'd treated her like a princess because of Thanos, then as a fighter because that was how they wanted her to die. Tonight proved, though, that there was nothing to stop them from treating her like much less. They would pile humiliation on top of humiliation, simply because they could, and if she fought back, they would finally have an excuse to simply execute her.

"I should have gone with my father," Ceres said, but she didn't really believe it. She couldn't run from what waited for her in the Stade, and she couldn't let her father take the risk of trying to break her out of there.

There was another option, of course. She might not be able to win, but she could deprive the nobles of their fun with her. One sweep of a knife across her wrists, and it would be over. Or she could stand there in the Stade and let it happen. She could refuse to give them the entertainment they demanded.

"Ceres?"

Ceres turned, recognizing the voice.

A woman stepped out of the darkness, and Ceres heart soared to see her old friend.

Anka. The girl she had saved from the slavers.

There appeared to be something tougher about her now that she'd joined the rebellion. Something less frightened of the world.

Ceres rushed forward to embrace her friend, the shock overcoming her.

Seeing Anka there was a shock. She'd been sure that she wouldn't see the young woman again. She was safe with the rebellion, or at least as safe as anyone could be with it. It was a good surprise though.

"How did you get here?" Ceres asked.

"It was hard getting in to see you," Anka said. "But there are things you need to know."

Something about her tone told Ceres what those things would be. "Rexus and Thanos are dead."

She said it as a fact, hoping to hear it refuted.

Anka paused. "You heard already?"

Ceres didn't want to say Stephania's name here. "One of the nobles here made sure I found out."

"That's—"

"Yes," Ceres said. "It is. You're sure though? They aren't lying?" She thought back to the moment when an arrow had struck Rexus as he was climbing, and he'd fallen through her hands, away into the depths below.

Anka shook her head. "I'm sorry, Ceres. We found the body. Rexus didn't survive the fall."

Pain shot through Ceres, clear and palpable. She should have guessed that it would be like this, but some part of her seemed to have assumed that Rexus would find a way to survive. There was something so powerful about him, so vibrant, that it seemed impossible anything could kill him.

"What about Thanos?" Ceres asked.

Anka shook her head. "We have friends around the fringes of the Empire's army. Some of them tell us that Thanos fell in the first assault on the beaches there, in the confusion as they fought to land."

That blow hurt even more than the news about Rexus. Perhaps it was just that there had been more hope. Ceres had seen Rexus fall, but Thanos... that could have been a lie designed to hurt her. Maybe it was more than that, though, and the thought of how much more made Ceres's stomach clench with the thought of it.

"It doesn't matter," she said. She shook her head. "None of it matters."

"You don't mean that," Anka replied.

"How can it matter when they're dead?" Ceres demanded. The idea that the world could go on without Rexus, without *Thanos*, just seemed impossible. "It doesn't matter. I'll be dead soon too."

Somehow, that felt like a relief. She wouldn't end things herself. No, she would do it the way that fate had set out for her. She would step out into the Stade, and she would die. She couldn't imagine it happening any other way now.

"The revolution needs you, Ceres," Anka insisted.

"No it doesn't," Ceres said. "Who has been running the revolution since Rexus died?"

"Well, I've been trying to get everyone to work together, but—"

"Then that's the answer. You don't need me, Anka."

Anka stepped back. "I don't know what to say. I never thought that you'd just give up like this."

Anger flashed through Ceres, and she welcomed it, because it seemed like the only thing that might replace the emptiness she felt right then. Her hands curled into fists. "Do you think I wanted this?" she demanded. "Do you think I wanted any of this? Do you think I wanted the man I love…" She trailed off, realizing what she was saying.

"I'm sorry," Anka said. "I didn't want to be the one to tell you all of this. And I thought I could try to get you out of here."

It was the same offer her father had made. Anka might even have the resources to do it if she could get there without any problems. Ceres knew her answer had to be the same, though.

"I can't go."

Anka took hold of Ceres's arm, pulling her toward the shadows. "You got me out of the slaver's cage. We both know all the things you saved me from. Do you know what it's like, knowing that you're going out into the Stade tomorrow to die?"

"I have to do this," Ceres insisted. "This is what I was meant to do, Anka."

"But we could get you out of here," Anka insisted.

Ceres disengaged the other woman's hand as gently as she could. "But it's not what I want."

Ceres heard a noise from the main hall and saw one of the doors opening. It was probably one of the nobles coming out to taunt her while she worked. Anka obviously heard it too, because she turned to slip back toward the darkness, beyond the spread of lamplight from the hall.

"This is your last chance," Anka said. "Please, Ceres."

Ceres shook her head, then called out as Anka started to go. "Anka, wait. If you want to do something that will help me, there is something."

"Anything I can," Anka promised.

"Help to make sure my brother and my father are safe," Ceres said. "The army took Sartes and my father is looking for him. They're both going to need all the help they can get." She held her hands earnestly as her friend prepared to flee, and she squeezed them.

"Can I trust you?" she asked.

Anka nodded back, with all solemnity.

"With my life," she replied. "Your family is my family, and I shall not stop until I find them—and bring them to safety."

CHAPTER TWELVE

Every step brought a wrench to Berin's heart as he traveled south, in search of the soldiers who had taken his son. Every step took him a little further from his daughter, left behind in a city where she would soon fight to the death. Every time his foot hit the ground, it felt like an impossible choice, one that he made only because his daughter had insisted.

Had he made a mistake?

Berin carried whatever supplies he could with him, their weight a constant on his back. Getting out of the city was easy enough, and after that he continued on the main roads for as long as he could. The roads were there for the army to march along, after all, so sticking to them seemed like the best way to find the unit that had taken his son. He only left them when he heard others coming, hiding by the side of the road until they passed each time. He didn't want to risk running into soldiers, bandits, or worse in these troubled times.

He came to a village after hours of walking, and it was easy to see that the army had been through there. It was too quiet, the way places were quiet in the wake of a storm. Berin had seen this before, in the years when he'd followed the army to smith for it. Armies devastated the country around them through the sheer numbers of men they contained, regardless of which side it represented. They stripped it bare whenever they stayed in one place too long, leaving the locals starving. A part of Berin suspected that the Empire sent out its army to take on foreign foes simply so that it wouldn't have to support it at home.

He hated the thought of Sartes being caught up in that. He wouldn't do well in the brutality of the Empire's forces. He wasn't cruel enough, or strong enough. The sooner Berin could get his son back, the better.

Berin could see a small market in the middle of the village, although there weren't very many stalls there now. Those that there were looked as though they only had scrapings left, with as many empty spaces on barrows and under awnings as there were goods for sale. Berin stopped at the nearly empty stall of a fruit seller.

"Has the army been through here?" he asked.

"Aye. Took half my stock as well, they did."

Berin nodded sympathetically. Times would probably be hard in the village for a while now, as the traders and the smallholders

53

tried to recover. Yet right then, it was hard for him to keep his attention on anything except what had happened to Sartes.

"Do you know which way they went?" Berin asked.

"Why? Going to join up?" The fruit seller asked that with a laugh that Berin made himself join in.

"Maybe. Although I think I'd be better off sticking to smithing."

"You're a smith?" the fruit seller said. "Then you should stay here. There would be plenty of work for you."

Berin shook his head, although there was a pang of regret that came with it. If there had been an offer like that a few months back, he might not have left his family. They could have found a spot in this village and been safe. Now, though, it was too late for that. "It's a good thought, but there are things I need to do."

He started to make his way around the rest of the market, always asking the same questions, always trying to make it sound as if he were just making conversation as he passed through. He spoke to tinkers and chandlers, butchers and farmers, getting the same picture from each of them: one of the army's units had been through a day or two ago, heading south to make camp.

Berin was asking a cheese seller if she knew anything when he saw the soldiers making their way through the market. He'd assumed that they would be long gone, but these must have been away on some errand. There were three of them, all leading horses. One wore the more elaborate armor of an officer, while the two beside him had the high boots and longer swords of cavalry. They were talking to the stall-holders, and though Berin couldn't make out the words, he could guess what they were talking about when the fruit seller pointed in his direction.

"Seems as though they're looking for you," the cheese seller asked him. "With all these questions, the others probably think that you're part of the rebellion."

"And the army left soldiers to watch," Berin said. He should have guessed that they would. His stomach knotted. He was afraid then, not for himself, but for Sartes. If he was caught, the soldiers would want to know what he was doing there, and if they found out that he was trying to get his son out of the army, then Sartes might be the one to pay the price. Berin couldn't let that happen, no matter what it took.

"Don't blame the others," the cheese seller said. "They're too afraid of the soldiers to do anything. *Are* you with the rebellion?"

To Berin, she sounded almost as though she was hoping that he was. That perhaps he was there to fight off the Empire's soldiers for them. That thought might have been laughable if the situation hadn't been so deadly serious. It was enough to make him take a risk. After all, what else did he have to lose?

"I'm trying to find my son," he said, and he saw the cheese seller's eyes widen. "He was taken away by the army as a conscript, and I want to get him back."

It was a big risk to take. He'd potentially just given this woman enough to condemn him, but some instinct made him trust her. Maybe it was just that he wanted to believe people would help, given the chance.

"I had a son once," the woman said. She nodded. "He starved two winters ago because the Empire had taken too much of our food for the city. Come with me."

She led the way away from her stall. Berin glanced back to see the three soldiers making their way across the market square, and he hurried after her. She led the way around the side of one of the village's small houses, to a space where linen hung out drying in the sun.

"Down that way," she said, pointing.

"Thank you," Berin replied. "I won't forget this."

He wanted to say more, but there was no time. Instead, he ducked amid the hanging washing, brushing it aside as he tried to lose himself in it. Somewhere behind him, he thought he heard soldiers shouting. He ignored it, concentrating on making his way through the village, staying in the shadow of the huts and outbuildings. He looked back and thought he caught a glimpse of an imperial uniform. He kept going.

Finally, Berin reached the edge of the village, where the houses gave way to the rising furrows of shared farmland. There was long grass along the side of the road, and he could have run easily then without being seen, but that wouldn't have helped him to get any closer to Sartes. Instead, Berin found a spot where he wouldn't be seen and hunkered down, putting aside the aches in his joints as he squatted there, waiting.

From his hiding place, Berin could see the soldiers out on the road. He held his breath as they looked out in his direction. If they caught him now, there would be no talking his way out of it. He'd run, and for them, that would be enough to prove his guilt. The best he could hope for would be a quick death. Berin stayed still, waiting as the men searched, then talked among themselves. After a while, they went back into the village, and one of the three came out riding his horse off at an angle from the road.

Berin started to follow the horseman, moving slowly, keeping low. When he passed out of sight, Berin switched to following the horse's tracks, and it was just as well the soldier had left a trail a blind man could follow, because Berin had never been much of a tracker. Despite the urgency of it all, he kept his head down and moved only at a walking pace. It was hard to be that cautious. Far more of him wanted to run to his son and rip him free from the army's clutches, but he couldn't help Sartes if he got himself captured, and the truth was that he couldn't keep up with the horseman even if he tried.

The flat ground gave way to a small rise with a stand of trees near the top. Berin made for them, pushing his way through the foliage and trying to watch where he put his feet so that he wouldn't make too much noise. As he reached the far side of the trees, he paused, freezing in place as he looked down.

There, spread out below, was the army camp. From up here, it was easy for Berin to see the grid pattern of the tents, the empty spaces left by the training areas and the clusters of wagons around the supply centers. He could see the fortifications around the edges too. There were rough ditches lined with spikes and built up with earth banks, watch platforms, and posts where dogs sat chained, there to sniff out intruders. Berin found himself wondering if they were there to keep would-be attackers out, or to keep conscripts in their place.

Sartes.

His son was down there somewhere, lost in that tent city, impossible to spot when everyone in it was dressed the same way. Sartes would be down among the conscripts, mistreated casually, because that was what the army did. Berin had to find him. He *would* find him, both because he wanted his family back, and because he'd promised Ceres. He would bring his son out of there.

He took the first step, knowing he would risk his life, knowing his chances of success were slim—and knowing he had no other choice.

CHAPTER THIRTEEN

Stephania moved quietly through the castle in the early morning. She doubted any of the other nobles who had been at the party last night would be awake yet. Lucious would certainly still be snoring. Normally, even Stephania would not have woken so early. This was an hour for servants and their chores, not for those who commanded them.

Under other circumstances she would probably have had her maid beaten for waking her. Only the contents of the message she had received had her padding through the corridors now in jeweled slippers.

In a way, it was probably a good thing that no one else was awake right now. Stephania wanted to do this without too many prying eyes.

She met the woman who had come in a small receiving room, barely large enough to accommodate the couch on which she sat. Stephania couldn't see her resemblance to Ceres, but even so, her servants had assured her that this was Ceres's mother. To Stephania, she looked like any other peasant woman, her dress stained, aging and lined, made hardened and coarse by her life. At least the woman had the grace to rise and drop into a curtsy as Stephania entered. Stephania doubted that her daughter ever would, even at sword point.

"You are the woman who came to the gate, claiming to be Ceres's mother?" Stephania asked.

"Yes, my lady," she said. "Marita, my lady."

She understood proper deference, at least. Stephania wasn't sure that she could ever like someone related to Ceres, but it made this easier. Stephania gestured for her to sit, joining her on the couch without ever quite sitting close enough that she had to touch her.

"Are you here because you wish to see your daughter?" Stephania asked, watching the woman carefully. It wasn't what the note had said, but Stephania was used to people lying. If a life at court had taught her one thing, it was that everybody lied. They lied for advantage, or to say what they thought people wanted to hear, or occasionally just because they wanted to cause trouble. Stephania had learned early to watch people carefully, to work out their real motives, and never to trust anyone.

Marita shook her head sharply though, and there was something about the sense of anger there that made Stephania want to believe the denial.

"I have no wish to see that... that *creature*," Marita said. "Not when she has cost me so much."

That was interesting, and not at all what Stephania had expected, in spite of the message. Stephania had expected greed perhaps, venality, but this level of hatred was... well, it was almost in line with her own.

"What did she do to you?" Stephania asked. It wasn't that there was the feeling of a kindred soul here, obviously. This woman could never be anything like a noble such as her. Even so, she had the same sense of Ceres having done something to harm them both. With her, it had been the disruption of her plans to marry Thanos. What had it been for this woman? Stephania wondered.

"She cost me everything," Marita said. "She cost me money that should have been mine. Money I got for her fairly! Then, when my husband found out, I was left with nothing!"

Briefly, Marita started to sob. Stephania sat and watched her for a second or two, gauging her there. Then she reached out to comfort the commoner, doing what she felt was a good job of hiding her distaste. Stephania was good at hiding what she felt, and who she was.

"That must have been hard," she said. She tried to keep her tone even. "When you say you got money for her, you mean you sold her to a slaver?"

"I had to get something for all the trouble she caused over the years," Marita insisted. Stephania could hear the defensiveness there. "My husband abandoned me, and she has always been difficult."

She paused as though expecting some sharp rebuke. Instead, Stephania patted her hand.

"I understand how difficult it must have been for you."

"It was!" Marita sounded almost shocked. "No one has realized that. My husband was so cruel. He shook me, and then he abandoned me! He just wanted to know where Ceres was, and our son Sartes."

Stephania already knew where they both were. They were exactly where they needed to be. Ceres would be dying in the Stade later today, while her brother wouldn't last long as a conscript. Briefly, she considered whether it would be worth getting rid of the mother as well, but no, she decided, that wouldn't do anything to exact justice from Ceres for what she'd done, and Stephania wasn't needlessly cruel.

"It sounds terrible," Stephania said. "No one should be abandoned by the one she is promised to."

That was one element of this woman's story that she could relate to. The pain when it had turned out that Thanos had been given to Ceres had been an icicle jabbed into her heart, the cold slowly spreading through her until there was nothing left.

"Why did you come here?" Stephania asked. "You said that you had information for me. Why bring it here though?"

"I thought someone should know," Marita said.

Stephania could see, though, that it wasn't the whole story.

"What else?" she asked.

Marita paused, looking embarrassed for a second. "When the slaver left with my daughter, he took all the money he gave me... I was *tricked.*"

"I understand," Stephania said. She'd brought a purse with her, even though it was early. She'd guessed that it might be necessary. Greed was one of the easier motivations to understand. It was also one of the more common ones. She pressed it into Marita's palm, closing her fingers around it. "Here. To help you now that your husband is gone."

She felt the way the other woman's hand clasped around it. Tightly, as if afraid it might be taken away at any moment. "You're too kind, my lady."

Stephania smiled back at her. "I don't think I've ever been called that before. Now, tell me what happened."

"After my husband left, I had nothing, so I went looking for Lord Blaku to see if I could get my money from him. He *owed* me." Marita had a note of determination in her voice that Stephania found quite amusing. She didn't know about this Lord Blaku, but she knew enough about slavers to guess what would have happened to this commoner if she'd found him.

"You went after him?" Stephania said. "Did you find him?"

The fact that she wasn't dead in some ditch said that she hadn't.

"I found what was left of him," Marita said. She shook her head. "He'd been killed, along with his men. At first I thought it was bandits, but bandits wouldn't leave this."

She took out a ring, more expensive than anything a commoner like her could have afforded. It had an ornate "B" insignia on the flat surface of the top, along with an insignia that might have pointed to a noble house. Stephania didn't have to ask why Ceres's mother hadn't sold it. It would be too obvious that it wasn't hers. The guards would have taken her in a heartbeat.

"That does seem unusual," Stephania said in her sweetest voice. "What would you guess happened?"

"I don't need to guess," Marita said. "I know. I asked around. I found one of the slaves they'd been transporting."

Stephania waited.

"My daughter killed Lord Blaku," Marita said. "Slaughtered him and his guards."

"Her alone?" Stephania asked. She wanted to be certain.

"That's what they said, although she must have had help," Marita said. That just told Stephania how little she knew her daughter. Stephania wasn't going to give Ceres much credit, but she could fight. If she couldn't, she would have been dead by now, and things would have been a lot easier.

"She killed Lord Blaku?" Stephania said. She lifted the slaver's ring up to eye level. Was it her imagination, or was there a smear of dried blood on it? It wasn't proof, not really, but what proof could there be for something like this? More to the point, how much proof would really be needed right now? If the story could be checked afterwards, if people could hear for themselves what Ceres had done, that might be enough.

"She did," Ceres's mother said. "I can point the spot out on a map, if you want."

"Yes," Stephania said. "I think that's a very good idea."

It shouldn't have mattered. Ceres would be dead soon anyway, if Lucious's man did his part in the Stade, but there was something unsatisfying about that. It was a heroic death, of the kind that people might talk about afterwards. Handled badly, Stephania suspected that it might even turn into a rallying cry for the rebellion.

This was potentially far better. If Ceres's mother had sold her, then she'd been a slave according to Delos's laws. If a slave killed their master, they could be killed and no one could question it. They could be flayed alive, whipped until they could stand no more of it, or simply strangled. They could take Ceres away for the kind of quiet death that would quickly fade from the mind, and any arguments could be quickly quashed.

Yes, let her have that kind of death. The kind of death that would inspire no one. Stephania stood, and Ceres's mother stood with her.

"What will you do with what I've told you?" Marita asked.

Stephania cocked her head to one side. "I'm going to make sure that your daughter gets exactly what she deserves."

60

Marita seemed to consider that. For a moment, Stephania thought that she might complain, or beg for some kind of leniency for Ceres.

Instead, to her shock, she nodded.

"Good," Marita said. "I should have strangled her at birth."

CHAPTER FOURTEEN

Ceres woke early, standing and stretching out her tired muscles in the morning sun, trying to pretend it was just another day.

Though she knew that it wasn't.

Her life would be at stake on this day. She would fight today, in front of thousands of spectators, against Lucious's combatlord.

That thought brought with it a kind of clarity, because it was obvious that Lucious was going to pit her against an opponent she couldn't beat. One that would ensure her death.

Ceres knew she should be afraid, but right then, she felt calmer than she'd thought she might. She half closed her eyes, feeling the warmth of the sun on her as she waited. The truth was that it didn't matter if she died today. Sartes would be safe, because her father and Anka were going to find him. Rexus was dead, but the rebellion would continue. As for Thanos…

Ceres forced herself to breathe as she thought of him being dead, letting the air out slowly as she tried to get back to the still place where she'd been. She wasn't sure she wanted to be alive in a world where he was gone.

Eventually, the guards came for her, hammering on the door in a way that made Ceres's ears ring after the silence. They put chains on her to march her down to the Stade, although Ceres had no intention of running away now. She saw the way the guards watched her now, with a kind of respect bordering on fear. They'd obviously seen her fight the first time.

She'd walked the route to the Stade plenty of times now to practice, but it felt different when it was for an actual fight. Part of that was the sound. Even here, the cheers of the crowd filtered through, making it feel to Ceres as though she was inside the belly of a living thing.

They reached the preparation room, and the guards removed her chains. To her surprise, one nodded.

"Good luck."

"Thank you," Ceres said. It was hard, sometimes, to remember that even the guards were people. Had this one seen her fight the last time? Ceres shook her head. She had to concentrate on getting herself ready for what was to come, but that felt impossible when her mind kept going back to other things. The last time she'd been in the Stade, how her father would be doing, Thanos…

Ceres stepped deeper into the preparation rooms. She didn't want to think about Thanos then, because it hurt too much. Paulo, her weapon-keeper, was waiting for her with her armor, a breastplate and kilt that left her limbs bare. Ceres knew that the idea was to have armor that protected the most vital areas of the body while still giving the crowd a chance to see blood on the sands. It made the fights last longer. As if in answer to that thought, Ceres heard the cheer that only came with the brutal end of violence. A minute later, the iron doors that led through to the Stade opened, letting guards drag a body back through. They abandoned it at the side of the room, probably expecting more to come.

"They tell me that you're fighting Lucious's man today," Paulo said.

Ceres nodded, reaching for her sword. "Do you know anything about him?"

Paulo looked uncomfortable, and Ceres could guess why he was suddenly quiet.

"It's all right," she said. "I'd rather hear it. I'm sure Master Isel would say that knowing an opponent is important."

Paulo smiled at that. "He says that you should know a foe like a brother." Ceres saw the smile vanish. "But he also says that victory is born from confidence."

Ceres understood. "It's all right. I want to know what I'm dealing with."

"The Last Breath," Paulo said, and Ceres could see the flicker of fear that crossed her weapon-keeper's face as he spoke about him. "He has been brought here from far to the south. He is larger than you, and stronger. He's fast, too."

Ceres shrugged. She'd guessed that he would be bigger than her. Most of the combatlords were. "The last man I fought was strong, too."

"Not like this," Paulo said. He shook his head. "The last time he fought in the Stade, he dropped his weapon, so he crushed his opponent's skull to finish him. But he's not just strong. The time before that, he fought Navencius. I've never seen anyone better with a trident than Navencius, but the Last Breath beat him in under a minute."

Ceres swallowed. She'd watched the killings enough to know how much that meant. Trident players were normally hard to get close to, the fights involving them becoming long games of cat and mouse. To kill one of the best with that weapon so quickly was more than impressive, it was frightening. Maybe Master Isel had been right. Maybe it was better not to know.

"So I should avoid the trident then?" Ceres joked.

Paulo didn't laugh though. Instead, he held out a sword in one hand and a long dagger in the other. "Better to stick to what you've trained with."

"A dagger though?" Ceres said. "Not a shield?"

"A shield would just make you want to stand still," Paulo said. "Trust me."

Ceres did. All the people around the Stade had become something like a second family for her, and Paulo knew what he was doing. She weighed the dagger in her hand. It was long enough to be a threat at more than close range, but short enough not to get in the way of her sword as she wielded it. It was a good choice. She waited with the weapons by her side, while beyond the preparation room, the sounds of the crowd built. Two more times, the guards came back with bodies, while three other combatlords limped back with wounds needing to be stitched.

Finally, it was her turn.

Ceres waited for the iron gates to open, then stepped out onto the sand, blinking as her eyes adjusted to the sunlight. The chanting of the crowd hit her in time to the beating of her heart.

"Ceres! Ceres!"

Last time, the words had seemed to run through her, building with her own excitement. Now, though, that excitement felt buried somewhere under everything that had happened. The feelings from the night before were still there. She was there to die. She knew it. With Thanos gone, she even welcomed it. But she wasn't going to give the royals the satisfaction of dying without a fight.

She stepped out into the middle of the Stade, looking around at the crowd. The terraced sides seemed even more crowded today than they would normally have been. Were those extra people there to see her? She looked over to the royal box, and sure enough, Lucious was there to watch. The others weren't there though, as though seeing the spectacle of her fighting were somehow beneath them.

Horns blared, and her heart froze as she saw her opponent step out onto the sands.

He was every bit as huge as Paulo had promised, his dark skin bulging with corded muscle and worked with tattoos. He wore almost no armor beyond a kilt and short greaves, as if ignoring the possibility of getting hit. For a weapon, he held a staff that had crescent-shaped blades on either end. He leaned on it without acknowledging the crowd. Even his weapon-keeper seemed to be frightened of him, following along behind at a safe distance and looking to Ceres as though he was ready to run at any moment.

On the edge of the royal box, an official in white stood and gestured for silence. In it, he boomed his announcement of the fight.

"For our next fight, we have the only woman to have ever fought in the Stade, the princess of the sands: Ceres!"

She stepped forward, waiting as the cheers rose to a crescendo. She should have been afraid, excited, something. Instead, the thoughts of what had happened to Rexus and Thanos seemed to consume everything else within her, drawing it down into some bottomless pit inside her. There was anger there though. Anger at everything the royals had done to her, and at the way this cruel world worked. A part of Ceres found itself welcoming the violence to come.

"Against her," the announcer continued, "we have Prince Lucious's greatest combatlord, the terror of the Stade: The Last Breath."

The Last Breath stood there, leaning on his weapon in what seemed to Ceres like contempt for the crowd. She wondered for a moment if he enjoyed any of this. Then he lifted his weapon and started to spin it. The bladed staff must have weighed more than either of Ceres's weapons, but her opponent twirled it as if it were nothing.

He spun it in arcs above his head, then out to either side. Ceres could hear the swish of the blades as they cut through the air, their rhythm like the scythe teams who cut meadow grass in the summer. He didn't watch the weapon as he spun it. Instead, Ceres saw his eyes fixed firmly on her. He brought the bladed staff around in one final arc, then swung it down to scatter the sand beneath his feet.

The crowd cheered at the display, but Ceres's opponent didn't react. His gaze didn't waver, and Ceres could feel the hostility there as his eyes bored into hers. She had the urge to take a step back then, or flinch, but she held herself still, concentrating on everything Master Isel had taught her. She could beat this opponent, but she had to move and keep moving.

Horns blared to signal the start of the contest. To Ceres, they seemed to come from a long way away. Even the crowd seemed to occupy a different space. There was only her and her opponent, crouched and waiting. The horn blast went on for several seconds, fading into echoes while Ceres waited.

Then the Last Breath leapt at her, almost too fast to follow, and Ceres knew the time had come to fight for her life.

CHAPTER FIFTEEN

By the time Stephania found the king and queen, they were already in the morning session of their court, listening to an argument about trading rights on the Empire's fringes. A fat merchant argued with one of the court's lesser nobles in front of them.

"And I say that I made all of the required payments," the merchant said. "But Lord Hywell has failed to pass them on to the Empire's revenue collectors."

"And is there any evidence of this?" the noble insisted. "Do you have any records of these payments?"

"Enough," King Claudius said. He pinched the bridge of his nose. "Do you think I want to listen to you prattle this early? Someone find the royal tax collector's records. If there is no record of the duty being paid, the merchant Zorat will pay it now, along with a fine of one part per hundred."

"But your majesty—"

The king's look was enough that even Stephania felt the urge to take a step back.

"You should be grateful," he said. "Trying to avoid the taxes of the Empire is normally punished with the gibbet. Which reminds me, when we find the royal tax collector, have him go through Lord Hywell's estate and find out just how much he has taken that should have been mine."

This time, it was the noble's turn to blanch. "I have always been loyal."

"Is it loyal to steal from your king?" the queen asked. "Take from the peasants if you must, but you do *not* steal from us. Now get out. Court is done for this morning."

"Wait, your majesties," Stephania called out. "I must be heard."

Almost everyone there turned to her. Most looked slightly shocked that anyone would dare to contradict the queen. Especially not when she and the king already seemed to be in a dangerous mood. Several stepped back, as though to distance themselves from whatever was going to come back.

"Stephania?" the queen said. "Do you think you can overrule our commands?"

Stephania swept down into her most perfect curtsy, keeping her eyes carefully downcast. She was sure she looked the perfect picture of elegant submission to royal authority.

"Forgive me, your majesties, but I have information that I believe you will wish to hear. Urgent information, relating to Ceres."

She looked up to see King Claudius looking straight at her.

"What about her?" the king asked. "She will die in the Stade today."

"If Lucious is right," Stephania said. She straightened up. "And even then, it is dangerous. The crowd might treat her as a hero when she dies."

Beside the king, Queen Athena drummed her fingers on the arms of her throne. "Weren't you one of the people suggesting that the Stade would be better than executing Ceres? Are you telling us that you advised us poorly, Stephania?"

Stephania thought quickly. "I argued against Ceres's execution out of hand, your majesty. The people would not stand for her simply being killed for no reason. But now, I believe I *have* a reason."

Stephania caught the change in atmosphere then. Feeling the mood of the court was an essential skill for anyone in her position. Now, she could feel it moving from being sharp edged and dangerous to something much more hopeful.

"What reason?" King Claudius asked.

Stephania took out the ring she'd gotten from Ceres's mother. She hadn't cleaned it, because the smear of blood on it seemed to make the whole thing much more convincing.

"This ring is from a slaver named Lord Blaku."

"I know of him," the queen said. "What is his role in this?"

It was a surprise to Stephania that the queen might know of a slaver, but then, the nobility made their money in all kinds of ways.

"He is dead, your majesty," Stephania said. "I have information that Ceres was the one who killed him, from the one who brought this ring."

"And who was that?" the queen asked.

"Her mother, your majesty," Stephania said. She risked a smile, because that was the part that clinched it. Anyone could make up an allegation, but for someone to be denounced by their own mother? That was practically impossible to ignore. "Ceres was the property of the slaver, and she killed him while escaping from him."

Stephania heard the faint intake of breath from some of the court. They clearly understood the seriousness of the crime. At this point, they could do almost anything they wished with Ceres and it would not matter.

King Claudius steepled his fingers. "What do you want us to do, Stephania? Wouldn't it be simpler to allow her to die in the Stade?"

"Simpler," Stephania said, "but perhaps not best."

"And you have something in mind instead?"

Stephania nodded. "I do, your majesty. The Isle of Prisoners."

That got another intake of breath and Stephania smiled at it. With all the punishments the Empire had, it seemed that the prospect of the Isle of Prisoners still had the power to shock. Stephania could understand that. It was a place of cruelty and punishment, from which few ever returned. Those who did returned broken and changed, as shadows of their former selves. Stephania looked around and watched them all start to understand.

"In the Stade," Stephania said, "Ceres is an embarrassment. At best, she is the girl we had to kill publicly because we hated her so much. She becomes a symbol that way. At worst... perhaps she will even continue to win."

"And that will become a different kind of symbol," Queen Athena said. "A symbol that people can resist us successfully. Hmm... Stephania has a point, Claudius."

The king sat there for what seemed like forever. Stephania could see him weighing it up, and someone else might have tried to say something then to push him in one direction or another. Lucious certainly would have, and Lucious would probably have found his king disagreeing with him, just to remind him of his place. Stephania had learned the lesson the noble petitioner before her hadn't. Sometimes, it was better to be patient.

"Yes," the king said at last. "I believe she does. It is a far better plan than Lucious's, at least."

Stephania smiled as sweetly as she could. "I am sure Lucious knows what he is doing."

Queen Athena regarded her carefully. "Even so, I think perhaps we have underestimated you in the past, Stephania."

"Oh, no, your majesty," Stephania said, even though it was undoubtedly true. "You have always been very kind. And this... well, Ceres's mother could have come to anyone."

"Yes, I suppose she could," the queen said.

Of course, Stephania thought, that would have required the others to pay attention and keep their ears open for useful information. Any of them *could* have done it. None of them did. But Stephania had no wish to appear too clever. It was better if they just thought she was lucky. Very, very lucky, in this case.

"What do you think should be done with Ceres once she reaches the Isle of Prisoners, though?" the king asked.

Stephania spread her hands. "A quiet death, your majesty. In whatever way pleases you most."

King Claudius nodded at that. "A quiet death, yes. A death that won't cause any more trouble."

"And a death where we can take our time," Queen Athena added. There was something cruel about the set of her features as she said it, but Stephania guessed that she could afford to be more open about it than Stephania was.

King Claudius seemed to be decided. "Yes, I like this idea. Go to the Stade, Stephania. See that Ceres is not killed where people will see her as a martyr. Let her disappear instead."

"Me, your majesty?" Stephania asked. She had expected them to send a servant, or their guards, or perhaps to go themselves. She hadn't wanted to be the one to end Lucious's fun directly. He was potentially a very useful ally.

"You are the one who suggested this, Stephania," Queen Athena said. "You should be the one to put it into practice. You will have our full authority."

And would no doubt be blamed if anything went wrong, Stephania thought. Still, the idea of the king and queen's full authority was a pleasant one. Stephania dropped down into another curtsy.

"Thank you for trusting me, your majesties. I will not let you down."

"I am sure you will not," Queen Athena said. "And if you do not, we will remember all the help you have given to us recently. Now go."

"At once, your majesty."

Stephania backed out of the smaller throne room, keeping to the courtesies required at court. It gave her enough time to enjoy the fact that things were going to go the way she wanted. When she reached the door, she turned and hurried through the corridors of the castle. The Killings would already be underway, the crowds of commoners cheering in their blood lust, and there would only be a little more time to fulfill the king and queen's orders. Stephania didn't want to think about what might happen if she failed.

Stephania went from a brisk walk to a run. She had never thought she would find herself doing this, but now she had to get to the Stade before Ceres was killed.

69

CHAPTER SIXTEEN

Ceres threw herself back just before a crescent-shaped blade flashed past her throat. The crowd roared, and instinct drove her to duck as the other end of the Last Breath's weapon thrust for her.

She tumbled across the sand, feeling it scrape across her skin as she came back to her feet, her adrenaline pumping with the intensity of the fight.

The crowd cheered.

Ceres stood there for a moment, trying to get her bearings as her opponent advanced on her—but there was no time. She parried another thrust with crossed blades, then felt the shaft of the staff slamming her back.

Again, the crowd roared.

Ceres retreated and circled, keeping her distance while she looked for a way past the whirling circle of half-moon edges. While those watching yelled for her to strike, she forced herself to breathe deeply, remembering her lessons.

Paulo had been right about her opponent's strength. Every time Ceres parried a stroke of the staff, the shock of it reverberated up her arms. Already, they ached with the effort of it, so that it felt as though all the strength she'd built in training was running out of her like water from a broken barrel.

She moved to her right, looking for a way to close the distance. She feinted with her sword, ducked under an answering sweep, and managed to scrape a cut across her opponent's arm with her dagger. Ceres heard the crowd chant her name.

A flash of sunlight on steel warned her about the counterstrike and she barely dodged back out of range again.

The Last Breath stood there, touched his arm, and lifted a bloody finger as if to examine it. He shrugged, and Ceres almost relaxed. Then he lunged forward again, blows coming for Ceres so fast she could barely see them.

Ceres parried the first three, tried to stab back, and felt the sudden pain along her leg as one of the blades cut across it. The clash of steel on steel came as another blow struck her breastplate, combined with an impact that spun her away, thankfully out of range of the next slash of blades.

Ceres saw the faint trail of droplets in the air as the spinning staff cast off her blood.

Ceres, desperate, kicked up sand toward the combatlord's eyes, trying to buy herself time. It rose in a cloud between them, briefly obscuring her view of her opponent. A crescent blade emerged from that cloud swinging around so fast that Ceres barely caught it.

Her sword snapped. Ceres had an instant to flinch as fragments flew; the blade sheared off just above the hilt, the shock of it sending a gasp through the crowd.

She threw the weapon at her opponent and tried to maneuver around so that Paulo could throw her a fresh weapon. The Last Breath seemed to have anticipated that, though, keeping between her and her weapon keeper, blocking any chance for Paulo to toss her the weighted net he was holding.

Ceres found herself waiting for the power that had come in her previous fights. She tried to summon it, but the truth was that she didn't have any idea how to. If she could find the power that she'd used to kill before, she might have a chance here.

But it didn't come.

For the first time in the Stade, she felt... ordinary. It was just her against this monster of a man.

The realization came to her, cold and hard in the pit of her stomach. She was going to lose. Ceres was surprised to find how much that meant to her. She'd thought she was at peace with it, ready, even eager to die. Yet now that it looked like she might, fear coiled around her, impossible to push back.

She managed to circle enough for Paulo to toss the weighted net to her. It wasn't a battlefield weapon the way a sword was. It was something designed for use in the Stade, so in that sense, maybe it was a good choice against an opponent from so far away, who might not have seen it before. A skilled fighter with it could tangle and trip, engulf and confuse an opponent. Ceres knew the theory of it, but she'd spent far less time with it than with the sword.

She kept her distance from the Last Breath, casting her net out in arcs that she tried to match to those of his bladed staff. Her only hope now was to wear him down, tangle his blades, and pull him in close to finish him. It was a desperate plan, and as the combatlord kept attacking, Ceres found herself retreating, step by step.

Around Ceres, the crowd booed. Where they'd called her name before, now she heard them catcall and hiss. Ceres knew how much the crowds at the Stade wanted action. They hated fighters who ran, yet right then, Ceres couldn't think of a better option. The Last Breath advanced on her, twirling his bladed staff, and backing up was the only way she could find to survive.

For a moment, the staff stalled, and Ceres saw her opening. She cast out her net, throwing it underhand so that it wrapped around the haft of her opponent's weapon again and again. The weights on the net locked it in place, as tightly as if Ceres had tied it there. Wrapping the trailing rope around her forearm, Ceres set her feet and pulled, trying to yank her opponent's weapon from him.

She saw the Last Breath smile as he stood there, steady as a rock.

He pulled back, and Ceres felt herself yanked forward. Too late, she realized the danger of gripping the net so tightly. Her opponent slammed the haft of his weapon forward as she stumbled in, and the weapon caught her just above the jaw. For a moment, the world seemed to swim, and Ceres tasted the iron tang of blood.

The combatlord struck her like that again and again, using the rough wood of the staff to pummel her head and body while Ceres stood trapped by her own grip on the net. Somewhere in that assault, she lost her hold on the dagger. Then the Last Breath kicked her, knocking her sprawling. Ceres could hear the crowds cheering again now, and they weren't cheering for her.

Ceres lay on her back in the sand. She wanted to get up, but there seemed to be a gap between thinking it and doing it that was too wide to cross. Instead, she could only watch as the Last Breath stood over her, seeming to blot out the sky above as he lifted his bladed staff for a killing blow. Ceres swallowed, anticipating the moment when he would bring it down, trying not to show any fear.

She heard a horn sound as if from a great distance, and managed to look over toward the royal box. She should have guessed Lucious would want to make this decision. It would be one final reminder for Ceres that her fate was in his hands. She looked over at the royal box and saw the noble standing there, his arm outstretched, while the crowd in the Stade called for life or death.

Far too many sounded as though they were calling for her death.

There was another figure in the royal box, though. It took Ceres a moment to recognize Stephania, and to realize that she was arguing with Lucious. Lucious was bright red with anger, his features twisted into something close to fury. Slowly, with obvious reluctance, he turned his thumb up for life.

Guards rushed out onto the sand. Several guided Ceres's opponent back in the direction of the iron gates. More seized her by the arms, lifting her between them so that her feet dragged on the ground. They fastened shackles to her wrists, not seeming to care about the way the iron bit into her. Ceres wanted to struggle as they dragged her away, but right then she didn't have the strength. She heard the boos of the crowd follow her from the Stade, down so that she could still hear them as they reached the practice rooms. She half expected to be unchained there, or perhaps to be dragged back to her chambers. Instead, the guards held her in place, still in her chains, until the door to the outside opened.

Stephania and Lucious came into the room together. Lucious still looked angry to Ceres, as though he couldn't accept that he'd been cheated of his chance to see her die. Stephania looked pleased, even triumphant.

"You should thank me for your life, Ceres," Stephania said. "After all, I did just save it."

"Why?" Ceres asked. She saw Stephania nod to the guards, and they shoved her roughly to her knees.

"You will speak to me with the proper deference, peasant," Stephania said. She paused. "No, you're not a peasant are you? You're a slave."

Ceres started to shake her head, but Lucious stepped forward and struck her.

"That felt good. If we had time, I'd do a lot more, slave. I couldn't believe it when Stephania told me what you were."

"But it's true," Stephania said. "And soon, everyone will hear it. Ceres here is a slave who murdered her owner."

"I was never owned by anyone," Ceres shot back. She could feel the anger rising in her. "Lord Blaku had no right to take me."

Stephania reached out to touch Ceres's cheek. "You think any of that matters? What matters is that you killed him. What matters is what people will *hear*."

Stephania stepped back toward the door, a vicious smile on her face.

"Your death won't be quick and valiant," Stephania said. "It will be slow, and painful, and anonymous. Say goodbye to Delos," she concluded, "and enjoy your trip to the Isle of Prisoners."

CHAPTER SEVENTEEN

Thanos cut his way toward the command post of the Empire's soldiers on Haylon. A soldier swung a blade at his head and Thanos ducked, striking out with his own weapon to bring the man down. Another ran at him and Thanos disarmed him, shoving him back into the melee around him. He fought and fought, never slowing.

Beside him Akila and his men fought hard, heading for the tents the Empire had erected on the edge of the city. They were easy to make out, because the Empire's standard hung above them, along with pennants proclaiming General Draco's presence.

With the Empire's ships gone, the battle for Haylon hadn't lasted long. Thanos had been right to guess that without their supplies and their siege weapons, their opponents would be at a disadvantage. The soldiers might have had the numbers, but they had no food and no safe places to sleep. They didn't know the island, and Akila's men were experts at springing from hidden spots to attack.

"Keep forward!" Thanos shouted, and to his surprise, the rebels responded. Since the attacks on the ships, there had been no more talk about killing him. Instead, they'd trusted him like one of their own. It had helped that Thanos had fought beside them against the soldiers who still remained, in skirmish after skirmish through a long night of fighting.

Thanos brought down another soldier, doing his best not to kill the man. Even now, it felt wrong to risk killing ordinary men who probably didn't have a lot of choice about being there. It felt wrong to be killing men who, as their prince, he should have been responsible for. Yet he kept going, because to stand back and let them take the island would have been worse.

"Getting tired yet, Prince?" Akila called out with a grin.

"I can keep going if you can," Thanos replied, although the truth was that he would have liked nothing better than to stop. It had been a long night of fighting, and now his sword felt as though it had been crafted from lead rather than steel. It was getting harder to swing by the moment.

He didn't have to keep going, though. The battle ended as swiftly as a summer storm lifting. Thanos saw the few remaining Empire soldiers between the rebels and the command tents throw down their weapons and run. The rebels surrounded the command tents, and less than a minute later, they dragged two figures from them.

General Draco walked straight-backed and proud, so that to Thanos, he looked as though he was marching out for a parade. He paused as he saw Thanos, and Thanos guessed that he was surprised to see him alive. That told Thanos a lot about how much he knew of the assassination attempt. The Typhoon was bloody and bruised, still fighting, but held in place by half a dozen men.

Thanos saw Akila looking over at him.

"You understand that we can't just let these ones live?" the rebel leader said. "After everything they've done to our city, we can't let them go."

Thanos understood what Akila was saying. He obviously thought Thanos would try to save the general and the Typhoon the way he'd tried to protect others. Thanos didn't answer. Instead, he stepped up close to General Draco.

"Draco."

"Thanos," the general said. "I'm surprised to see you alive."

"I'm harder to kill than that," Thanos said.

The general shrugged. There was an edge of fatalism about it. "I take it that the capture of our ships was due to you? I heard reports, but I wouldn't have thought you'd be ruthless enough to fire on your own side. You were quite squeamish before, I recall."

Thanos's hand tightened around the hilt of his sword. "You commanded the deaths of women and children. You encouraged your soldiers to rape and pillage. I don't like killing, but the world is better off without you."

The general looked as though he might say something else, but Thanos didn't give him an opportunity. He did it quickly, before he could stop himself. He thrust up, into the general's throat and out again, stepping back while Draco stared at him in obvious shock. The general collapsed to his knees, then tumbled forward into the dirt. Thanos moved over to the Typhoon.

"Who ordered you to kill me?" he asked.

The Typhoon stared at him. "You'll let me live if I tell you?"

"No," Thanos said. "You're going to die for all the evil you've done here. You're going to die for trying to kill me. But at least you can die with some honor."

"What would you know about honor, traitor?" the Typhoon demanded.

Thanos struck out again, this time in a lateral sweep that ended with the huge soldier's head rolling to the floor. Thanos let his sword fall to land point first in the earth. He should have felt satisfaction at this, or elation at the victory, but as it was it just felt as though a grim chore was complete.

75

"It seems I didn't have to worry about you after all," Akila said, coming forward to clap Thanos on the shoulder. "Well done. Without you, Haylon would have fallen to the Empire by now."

That was a good thing to be reminded of as Thanos looked out over the death and destruction he'd been a part of. It meant that he could look toward Haylon, where there were fires still burning, and think that it was all worth it.

"I did what I needed to do," Thanos said.

"You did more than that," Akila assured him. "You acted the way a true friend would, and we will always think of you that way. No, as more than that. As a brother."

He embraced Thanos, and Thanos didn't know what to say. He hadn't been trying to do anything special. He'd just been trying to do the right thing for the people of Haylon. For free people.

"What now?" Thanos asked. "More ambushes?"

Akila shook his head. "If the Empire soldiers want to run, let them. As for what happens next… well, I was going to ask you that, Prince. Me and my boys owe you a lot, so what do you want to do now?"

Thanos stood there, looking over at the tents while he tried to make up his mind. The sea breeze washed away some of the smell of death that surrounded him, but not all of it. Not by a long way.

What did he want? For the past couple of days, it felt as though he'd been running on instinct. Now, though, there was a moment to think, to pause, and to feel. The last part of it was easy, at least. For what seemed like the first time in his life, he knew exactly what he felt.

He stepped forward and grabbed a handful of the Empire's standard, yanking it down.

"I want revenge," he said. "I've tried so hard to be the kind of prince the Empire needed, and they tried to kill me for it. I want to find out who ordered that."

"Is that all you want?" Akila asked him.

Thanos shook his head. It wasn't the only thing. Not by a long way. "I want to find a way to make it stop. They've spent their lives hurting the people they're meant to be ruling on behalf of, building palaces and taking from them. I want to march in there and tear it down around them. I want to change the way the regime treats the people. I want to make sure that people like you are free forever…And I want to see Ceres."

That burned brighter in him than all the rest of it put together. When he'd thought he was dying, she was what he'd thought of, and now he wanted nothing more than to be able to pull her into his arms. He didn't care what it took, he needed to get back to her.

"I want to lead your men into the middle of Delos, take the city, and not stop until we've wiped away every cruelty in the Empire," Thanos said.

"You sound determined," Akila replied.

Thanos was. In that moment, he could have torn down the entire ruling family and led the assault on Delos himself. He saw the rebel leader shake his head though.

"Even if I could persuade my lads to march on Delos now," Akila said, "it isn't the right time for it. The Empire is still strong, and the nobles' grip on it is too firm. This will take more than an army marching in to solve it."

"What will it take then?" Thanos demanded. "I can't just sit here and do nothing, Akila."

"You won't have to," Akila promised. "But perhaps you can do more good inside Delos's court than you can marching on it."

It took Thanos a moment to understand. "You want me to be a spy for you?"

Akila nodded. "You're the one man who might have a chance to work for our interests on the inside. You can tell them that you survived the fighting. It might give you a chance to find out everything you want to, and you can warn us if King Claudius wants to send more men to Haylon."

It made sense, but even so, it was hard. Thanos didn't like playing the games of court at the best of times. Being there as a spy would only make it worse. He wanted to march in and take his vengeance directly. But the truth was that he didn't even know who had ordered his death. This might give him a chance to find out, to pave the way for the rebellion...

...and to see Ceres.

That thought was the one that decided it for Thanos. If he could see Ceres again, then the rest of it would be worth it. He could put up with any amount of subterfuge and politics if she was there, and the thought of her waiting was enough to make him want to rush home.

"How will I even get back?" Thanos asked.

"Leave that to us," Akila said.

It took time, and in that time, the rebels celebrated him. They set fires where the Empire's tents had been, and those quickly became the center points of a feast. The rebels danced and drank, ate and congratulated one another. Thanos found himself at the heart of it all, unable to go more than a minute or two without one of the rebels clapping him on the back or offering him wine.

They found him a small boat, in the end, with a couple of fishermen from Haylon to crew it. The boat he'd come in on was gone, lost in the fires the rebels had set, but at least this one looked as though it could make the journey. Akila's men packed it with food and supplies, lining up on the beach to cheer as Thanos boarded.

"Thanos! Thanos!"

Thanos stood there watching them, and he would never have thought that this would feel as if he were leaving a family. He was supposedly going home, but right then, this was the place that felt like home. He watched Akila waving on the sand and Thanos saluted him with his sword, one warrior to another.

He felt the boat lurch as it started to move away. Thanos watched until Akila's men were out of sight, but quickly turned his thoughts to Delos, and everything he would have to do once he got there. It would be dangerous, perhaps more dangerous than anything else he'd done. All of it would be worth it, though, for one simple reason:

He was going to see Ceres again.

CHAPTER EIGHTEEN

Ceres stumbled in blackness as they marched her toward the prison ship. Around her, she could hear the jibes and insults of the people she passed. She couldn't see them, but she could hear their sudden hate and contempt, pouring over her like water in a storm.

Ceres flinched as something struck her, bouncing off her breastplate. It might have been a piece of fruit or a stone, she didn't know which. Unable to see it and held in place as she was, there was no chance for her to dodge it. Her breastplate and kilt offered some protection, but really just meant that she was easier for the crowd to identify.

"Murderer!"

"Slave!"

The hardest part was hearing the anger in voices that had been calling her name in the Stade just a little while before. Ceres knew that the royals must have started their rumors and their announcements even before her fight in the Stade was finished, because that was the only way it could have spread so quickly.

She felt the pull of metal against her wrists as the guards dragged her along by the shackles that held her. Ceres didn't fight the movement, but she felt their sudden yanks and jerks against the chains anyway. She heard people laugh as she stumbled, and Ceres knew that was the point. They wanted her humiliated.

Finally they came to a halt, and the guards dragged the hood from her head, leaving her blinking back tears in sunlight that seemed blindingly bright after the darkness before.

A huge shape stood before her, and it took a moment for Ceres to make out the detail of the ship that sat there. It was an ugly hulk of a thing, bulky and round, tattered and with rusting fittings. The prison ship seemed to be designed to hint at the horrors to come on the Isle of Prisoners, even its gangplank seeming like the spine of some long dead creature.

They dragged Ceres up it, and she walked with shuffling steps. She had enough time to look back and see the crowds there, looking out over the sea of angry faces, all there to show their hatred of her. Was it because of the things the royals had said about her, or because she'd lost, or both? She didn't know.

The gangplank seemed to stretch out forever. Ceres thought about diving from it into the water below, but chained as she was, she would sink instantly, even if she could break away from the guards' grip.

Her footsteps seemed to shake it, and for a moment Ceres thought that she might tip in anyway. She felt the guards tighten their grips on her and throw her forward, so that she landed on the rough wood of the deck. Above her, black-stained sails lay furled on their masts, while she saw sailors lounging on the deck, watching her the way the crowds had below.

Ceres pulled herself to her feet, but the guards took a grip on her again. They dragged her toward an iron-barred hatch, open to the sky, then threw her through it, so that she stumbled down the steps below. She tried to curl and roll to keep from being hurt, but even so, the impact jarred her.

The first thing to hit her was the smell of too many people pressed together too close, the stink of it sharp and acrid with sweat. There were people huddled down there in shackles and chains. Ceres could see men, women, and children thrown together, with no apparent order or care. Some were attached together in long coffles, while others were bolted to the walls. Ceres found herself wondering where they had all come from, and what they had done.

Ceres looked up toward the hatch, just in time for one of the guards to spit down after her in contempt.

"Better get comfortable. The Isle of Prisoners will be a whole lot worse."

***

Ceres didn't dare sleep as the prison ship rolled and bucked its way across the sea. Instead, she sat watching the other prisoners there, trying to project a sense of strength that would keep the more dangerous ones at bay.

It was a cruel place. Some of those there were probably perfectly normal people: members of the rebellion the Empire didn't want to kill too quickly, people who had stolen to feed their families, or who had found themselves on the wrong side of the court's political games. There were others, though, who were far more dangerous. Since she'd been there, Ceres had heard one man boasting about the number of people he'd killed, while there had been another screaming and raging for no apparent reason. Already, Ceres had seen fights, murders, and more down there.

As far as she could tell, the guards had no interest in stopping any of it. When they brought food, they threw it out at random for the people there to fight over. Ceres managed to grab a hunk of bread that landed near her, but there were others who were not so lucky. She saw one man in the faded clothes of a noble being beaten for a crust, the gold brocade on his tunic being ripped away simply because it might have some value. This place seemed to have no rules beyond the strongest taking what they wanted. The violence of the place was enough to make Ceres feel sick that people could treat one another that way.

So Ceres forced her eyes to stay open, trying to keep her back to the bulkhead of the ship, where she could see all the others around her. She was still watching when she saw the girl.

She was young, probably around ten years old or so, and painfully thin. Her dress was torn, and her face smeared with dirt. Her sandy blonde hair was so tangled and dust streaked that it looked brown in places. She was currently crawling along, trying to snatch food from the edges of the melee without being seen.

She didn't succeed. Ceres saw a large, scarred man turn on her, raising up to his full height.

"What do you think you're doing? Give me that! Scrawny little brat, I'll kill you!"

He took a step forward, and Ceres couldn't hold herself in place. She sprang in between the girl and her would-be attacker, hands up ready to fight.

"Leave her alone," Ceres said.

"I'll do what I want," the thug said. Ceres saw him look her up and down. "To her, and you."

Ceres felt anger rising in her. Energy rose in its wake, flooding through her. Her opponent charged at her, but she was already moving. She sidestepped the thug's rush, leaving her foot out to trip him. As he went down, she was already on him, the chain that connected her shackles wrapping tight around his throat. She heard him make a gurgling sound as she strangled him, before he fell still.

She could have kept going. She could have choked him until he died, or pulled until his neck snapped. It would have been the kind of message the rest of the hold would understand. Instead, Ceres let go, kicking the man's unconscious body away.

She saw several of the hold's other denizens descend on him to rob him. Ceres held back her disgust and went back to her spot instead. The girl was there, obviously not wanting to move too far away from her. Even so, she looked frightened, as though expecting Ceres to lash out at her at any moment.

"It's all right," Ceres said. "I'm not going to hurt you. I'm Ceres."

The girl took a moment to consider that, and Ceres guessed that she was trying to work out all the ways the conversation could go. "I'm Eike."

81

Ceres held out a small piece of bread to her, and Eike took it, staring at it for a moment before biting down hungrily. She looked up at Ceres, as though waiting for what it would cost her. Ceres gestured to the patch of deck beside her.

"You can sit down if you like," Ceres said.

"Do I have to?" Eike asked.

"You don't have to do anything you don't want."

The girl snorted. "I know that's not true here."

Even so, she sat down. She watched Ceres with obvious curiosity.

"Is it true that you fought in the Stade?" she asked eventually.

Ceres nodded. "That's right."

"Is it true that you killed your master, too?" Eike asked. Apparently the rumors had made their way here, too. "They say that's why you're here."

"I killed a slaver who tried to capture me, and who had a knife to my friend's throat," Ceres said.

Eike stared back.

"I am here because my family joined the rebellion," she said. "When the soldiers came, they took all of us. Now"—she choked back a sob—"I'm the only one left."

Ceres put an arm around her. She felt Eike tense like an animal ready to run, and that just made her feel worse for her. No one that young should be stuck somewhere like this. Ceres didn't want to think about what they would do to the girl on the Isle of Prisoners.

She didn't want to think about what they would do to her, either. The Isle had an evil reputation as a place of torturers and cruel deaths, oubliettes and mass cages. Once there, there was almost no coming back, certainly not for anyone like her. A quick death in the Stade would have been better, Ceres decided. Far better.

"If you want to sleep, I could keep watch," Eike offered.

Ceres looked over to her. She guessed that the girl was looking for a way to make herself useful so that Ceres wouldn't abandon her. Ceres wouldn't do that, but in this place, it would be hard to convince her that anyone was capable of acting out of altruism. Besides, she was currently so exhausted that the idea of being able to sleep meant almost as much as freedom would have.

"I'd like that," Ceres admitted. "Wake me if there's trouble."

"There's always trouble," Eike said. "But I'll wake you up if anyone comes close."

It seemed bizarre to Ceres to be trusting her safety to this girl, but the exhaustion of her day overcame her, and before she could think twice, the rocking was already lulling her heavy eyes to sleep.

CHAPTER NINETEEN

Lucious was in a mood to celebrate. He threw back a goblet of wine too fast, raising it in a mocking toast to thin air as it burned in his throat.

"To vanquished irritants!"

He tossed the goblet casually at a servant, and the man scrambled to catch it, probably terrified that Lucious would have him beaten if he let it hit the floor. Lucious resolved to have him beaten later anyway, just to keep the man on his toes.

He made his way in the direction of the throne room. Ordinarily, he found the business of the court boring, but perhaps today it would turn to more of a party atmosphere. The problem was dealt with, and soon it would be the Festival of the Moon, one of the biggest festivals in Delos's calendar. Normally, that meant days of feasting and parties, presents and enjoyment. The feasts at the castle were always a lavish affair.

Lucious was halfway to the throne room when he saw the older woman arguing with the guards.

"But Lady Stephania promised me! I was the one who gave her Ceres!"

Lucious stepped across to the argument, looking the woman over. To him, she looked nondescript and worn, not worth his interest. Only Ceres's name caught his attention.

"What's going on here?" he asked.

"She wants to speak to Lady Stephania," one of the guards said.

"I'm owed," the woman said. She held up a pouch, clutched so tightly Lucious could see her knuckles sticking out. "She gave me money for what I knew about Ceres, but now that it's let her get rid of my daughter—"

"Your daughter?" Lucious said. Despite the wine, that got through. "You're Ceres's mother?"

"I am." The woman seemed to remember herself enough to curtsy. "Marita, my lord. I provided the information that let them take Ceres."

"So you're the reason I didn't get to see her die in the Stade?" Lucious asked, letting a brief note of anger seep into his voice. That was the one part of this that still rankled. That his carefully prepared plan could be set aside, and Stephania's could work so well instead. Everybody knew that she was just a vacuous ornament at court, but through some stroke of luck she'd succeeded.

Ceres's mother looked frightened at that. She was right to be.

"And now you're here for more money?" Lucious said. He shook his head. "That's just… ungrateful."

The woman seemed to understand the position she'd put herself in at last. "I… I'll go."

"Not yet," Lucious said. He grabbed the coin pouch, ripping it from her hand and then tossing it to one of the guards.

"That's mine!" Ceres's mother insisted.

"It *was* yours," Lucious said. "Now it is this guard's."

"I earned that!" the woman insisted.

Lucious snapped his fingers. "She needs to learn the price of getting above her station. Take her outside, and take everything of value she has. Then throw her in the gutter like the trash she is."

"Yes, Prince Lucious," the guard said.

"No!" Marita screamed as the guards grabbed her by the arms. "You can't do this to me!"

It always amused Lucious when peasants tried to tell him what he couldn't do. They didn't understand how the world worked. He stood and watched as the guards dragged her outside, then called out, almost as an afterthought.

"If she resists, beat her until she learns better."

Lucious smiled then and headed for the throne room. The others were already there, and as he'd predicted, it had something of a carnival atmosphere to it. He could see Stephania at the heart of a clique of the other noble girls, with them fawning over her as usual. The king and queen sat on their thrones while before them, nobles chattered and congratulated themselves on having dealt with the crisis. Probably half of them were busy trying to claim credit for the outcome.

Lucious made his way through them, and today they mostly stepped back to give him room to get through. Many of the more minor nobles bowed or nodded, giving him the acknowledgment he deserved.

"Lucious, would you like to come to a gathering we're having for the Festival of the Moon?" one of the young noblewomen there asked as he passed. "We have a group of masked players this year who are simply delightful."

Another cut in straightaway. "Masked players are *so* last year. We have tumblers brought from the far south, and perfumers who have promised clouds of scented smoke."

"Tumblers?" the first said. "And I suppose you'll be serving the same quails and oxen as last year as well?"

Lucious forced a smile. The truth was that he would go wherever they treated him most like the prince he was on festival night. He would probably tour from party to party until they all blended into one.

"It sounds good," Lucious said. "I'll think about it."

More offers followed as he continued through the crowd.

He was almost to the front when King Claudius stood up, raising his hand for silence and instantly bringing the chattering to a halt. He stood there, and despite his age, Lucious could see the power there within him.

"Why are you all so happy?" he demanded. "Because we have gotten rid of one girl?"

"And killed the leader of the rebellion," Lucious pointed out. "Rexus is dead. Ceres is gone. The people have no one to lead them."

"That is true," Queen Athena said. "The rebellion is hurt, but that does not mean that our people will settle back into their lives easily."

"They must be *pressed* back," King Claudius said, "and firmly!"

Lucious suspected that he knew where this was going. The king and queen had ordered periods of greater severity before. Lucious had never understood why it was necessary to order it. Surely, no unrest or disobedience should ever be tolerated?

"How are they to be pressed back, your majesties?" Lucious asked. He guessed that it was the question on the minds of most of those there. Well, those who weren't preoccupied with how to host the most out of control party for the festival, at least. Stephania, for example, seemed utterly uninterested, more concerned with the attention of her coterie of noblewomen. "How much more can be done?"

Queen Athena gave him a hard look. "You don't believe that we have a plan, Lucious?"

"I'm sure you do, my queen," Lucious said. "I'm just eager to hear what it is. I'm sure we all are."

More likely, everyone there wanted to know whether it would affect them. He thought back to some of the things they had tried in the past. Those with rebel sympathies had been rounded up and either killed or enslaved. Their families had been imprisoned, their homes burned. There had been harsh taxes and harsher methods of collection. It had seemed obvious to Lucious that eventually they would realize that they were bringing such measures on themselves with their defiance, but curiously, the more rebels they treated harshly, the more there seemed to be. There was no logic to it, but then, who understood how the lower orders thought?

"I have heard you all talking about the Festival of the Moon," King Claudius said. "Well, I believe that it is appropriate that our Empire makes its rulers an offering for the festival, in reparation for all the trouble the rebellion has caused."

"What kind of offering?" Lucious asked.

King Claudius shrugged. "Whatever we desire. From now until I decide that the people of Delos have learned the price of resistance, any noble will be able to take whatever they wish from the rest. If you want their children as slaves, they are yours. If you want their last coins, or the clothes off their backs, they will give them. They say we have taken too much from them? We will move among them and show them what it is like to have *everything* taken from them."

"There will be those who resist," Lucious pointed out.

"You sound as though you're arguing against our command, Lucious," Queen Athena said.

Lucious shook his head. "Not at all, your majesties. I'm merely asking what I am permitted to do when they *do* fight back."

He heard the slap of flesh on flesh as the king slammed his fist into his palm. "Crush them. Kill any who refuse to hand over what is ours. Remind them that they only own anything in this Empire through our grace. Slaughter them, enslave their families, and have their neighbors watch as you take everything they have ever owned."

Lucious smiled at the thought of that. It was the kind of thing he'd done with Ceres's mother, only on a scale that would encompass the whole Empire. Perhaps some would argue, perhaps some would fight, but they would only serve as examples for the others.

"I would like to lead these efforts," Lucious said, thinking with relish of the possibilities.

Queen Athena smiled. "We thought you would, and we think you're the perfect choice. Go out among them, Lucious. Take our guards with you, and make them properly afraid of their rulers for once."

"With pleasure," Lucious said, and it would be a pleasure. It wasn't so much the thought of everything he could take from the peasants as the act of taking itself. He was sure that there would be the opportunity to show plenty of them their place in ways they would never forget. "When do you want me to begin?"

"At once," King Claudius said. "I want this to be a Festival of the Moon that all of Delos will remember."

"Oh, it will be," Lucious promised. "It will be."

CHAPTER TWENTY

When Thanos returned to Delos, there were guards on the docks—indeed, there were guards everywhere. The whole city had the feel of a place under siege, making it hard to tell the difference between the Empire's capital and the way Haylon had been when it was under attack. He saw bones hanging in a gibbet over the water, the iron chain that held it creaking as it moved in the wind.

A part of Thanos wanted to avoid the guards. They reminded him too much of the soldiers he'd fought back on the rebels' island. Yet he needed to play the part of the loyal prince, returning from the war, and that meant not sneaking around.

"You there," he said to the first group he found. They appeared to be engaged in stripping a waterfront home of its contents. "What are you doing?"

"Enforcing the orders of the king," their sergeant said. "What's it to you?"

"I am Prince Thanos. You will stop this and escort me to the castle at once."

He saw the guards pale at that, but they did as he commanded. Thanos looked around as they walked with him back to the castle. In the time he'd been away, it seemed that plenty had changed. He could see other groups of soldiers looting houses, while more gibbets hung on street corners. Some of the occupants were still alive. Graffiti scrawled on the walls proclaimed the cruelty of the king among the more usual comments on the fighters in the Stade. Just the thought of them had him thinking about Ceres.

By the time he reached the castle, it was hard to concentrate on anything else, but Thanos knew he had to. He had to keep up the pretense of loyalty, the illusion of being the perfect prince. One slip could mean more than his life. It might mean defeat for the rebels' plans too. He had to find out who had ordered his death, and look for ways to help the rebels. Despite all of that, the urge to see Ceres was almost more than he could bear.

He could have gone to his old rooms and changed before heading for the throne room. Instead, Thanos strode in as he was. He wanted everyone there to see him with the dirt and blood of the conflict for Haylon on him. He wanted them to understand what had happened there. He stepped into the throne room, and heard the collective gasp from those there.

They stood in place as if frozen. Thanos walked forward between them, letting his eyes flicker left and right. He could see plenty of nobles he knew there, all looking as though they were dressed for a celebration. He spotted Cosmas in a corner, the scholar looking as though he was making mental notes on everything that was happening in the room. Lucious was off to one side, in grand armor that made him look like the general of an invading army. Stephania was holding a peach, just poised to take a delicate bite out of it. At the head of the room, King Claudius sat on his throne, while Queen Athena had moved off among the nobles to talk to them.

Thanos took all that in, and he slipped through the crowds toward the throne. Once he reached the dais, he fell to one knee, bowing his head as if in shame.

"Your majesty, I regret to inform you that the expedition to retake Haylon has not been a success."

It was an understatement. If the king knew anything about what had happened, he would know it had been a disaster. Briefly, tension clamped around Thanos. What if soldiers had escaped back to Delos? What if a dove had returned with a message? The king might already know about the part he'd played in the destruction of the Empire's forces.

The room was silent for several seconds. In it, Thanos found his thoughts of possible discovery swept away by the need to examine the others there. Someone had sent an assassin for him. He would find out who had done that.

"Thanos?" the king said, standing. He took Thanos's hands, drawing him up to his feet. To Thanos, it seemed like a surprisingly tender gesture, given how cruel the king usually was. "You're alive? We heard that you were killed by the rebels on the beaches of Haylon."

Thanos tried to listen for the nuances of that. Was the king disappointed? Had he been the one to send the Typhoon with orders to kill him?

"I was almost killed, though it wasn't by rebels," Thanos said. "One of our own soldiers stabbed me in the back."

He looked around at the room as he said it. Did anyone look shocked by the revelation? Did anyone look satisfied? How many of those here could have bribed or commanded the Typhoon? The truth was that it was too many. There was almost no one there he could trust. Every smile at his return was as likely to be fake as real.

"One of our own betrayed you?" the king said. "Why?"

"He claimed to be sent by someone at court," Thanos said. Again, he heard a gasp go around the room. "Although he wouldn't say by whom."

"How did you survive?" the king asked.

"I was left for dead," Thanos said. "Fishermen found me, and brought me back when they realized who I was. They thought there would be a reward."

It was the kind of lie he guessed the others there would believe. They understood greed far better than kindness, in Thanos's experience. He paused. It was going to be hard lying constantly. He'd tried to build his life on honesty…

…and that had nearly gotten him killed.

"And my army?" the king asked.

"I heard the fishermen talking. They said that the Imperial fleet had been burned, the land forces cut off. I'm sorry, your majesty, but I believe General Draco is dead."

King Claudius looked at him for a long time. Thanos found himself wondering how much of his story the king believed. He spent his life with courtiers telling him half-truths and outright lies. The only thing protecting Thanos now was the fact that he'd never lied to his king in the past.

"A terrible loss," King Claudius said. "But I am more concerned with the fact that you were attacked. Every aid will be provided in finding the one responsible. If there is anything you require, you have only to ask."

"Thank you, your majesty," Thanos said, although he had no intention of simply relying on the king's efforts. There was one thing the king could give him, though. "May I be permitted to see Ceres?"

That made the king's expression change. It went from something that looked like genuine concern to anger almost as fast as Thanos could blink.

"All of this, and your mind is still on that girl?"

It always would be. Thanos found himself thinking of Ceres as she'd been when he'd left, angry with him for the betrayal of fighting against the rebellion. If he could whisper the truth to her…

"I would like to see her," Thanos said.

"That is not possible," Queen Athena said. "The girl is gone."

Thanos spun to her. "Gone? What do you mean 'gone'?"

"Mind your tone, Thanos," King Claudius said. "What you have been through gives you some leeway, but remember where you are."

The queen gave him an answer, though. "Your precious Ceres turned out not to be all she seemed. She was a slave who had killed her master, not fit to live, let alone fight in the Stade. As we speak, she is on a ship headed for the Isle of Prisoners."

The queen seemed to take a certain cruel delight in telling him that. She smiled as Thanos reeled before the news, and it was all he could do not to start shouting. He wanted to demand Ceres's return; to charge down to the docks and set off after her on whatever boat he could find. As it was, he found that he couldn't bear to stay there any longer. Between the people who'd tried to kill him, the ones who'd gotten rid of Ceres, and the usual poisonous atmosphere of the court, how had he thought that he could stand to be here without exploding?

Somehow, Thanos managed to keep enough of a grip on himself to force a bow. "Forgive me, your majesties. My wound is paining me, and it has been a long journey. With your permission, I would like to retire to my room."

"Yes," King Claudius said. "Perhaps that is a good idea."

Thanos hurried from the throne room, and he saw the courtiers there rush to get out of his way. He didn't know what they saw in his face, but they stepped back quickly, leaving a clear route to the door. Thanos had made it out into an antechamber before he felt a hand on his shoulder.

He spun, his anger rising. If someone wanted to stop him now, in the moments after he'd learned that he'd lost Ceres, then—

"Prince Thanos," Cosmas said, taking a step back. The old scholar looked much as he always had to Thanos: spry despite his age, bald, with pronounced ears and a beak of a nose that only seemed to draw attention up to the intense blue of his eyes.

"Cosmas," Thanos said. The old man's presence was enough to calm him a little, but only a little. "I'm sorry. I can't talk now. Ceres—"

"I know, boy," the scholar said. "Some pains are too much to deal with all at once. You came back thinking of a happy reunion, and it hurts to have that dashed."

It did more than hurt. It felt as though something in Thanos was tearing itself apart. Even so, he nodded.

"I need some time alone," he said.

"I understand," Cosmas replied. "But when you are ready, we need to talk."

"Why?" Thanos asked.

"Because I believe I know who tried to kill you."

CHAPTER TWENTY ONE

Ceres was resting when the ship lurched. She was on the edge of sleep with Eike near to her, and she barely had time to wake up before she was rolling as the ship listed. She only kept from tumbling right across the deck by grabbing for one of the long chains that bound prisoners in place.

It had to be a storm, and a big one too if it could rock the ship like this. Beside her, Eike grabbed hold of the same chain, and Ceres moved closer to wrap her arms around the girl, climbing along the chain until she could do it. As small as the girl was, there was no way she would survive if she found herself thrown across the hold of the ship.

Several of those prisoners who weren't chained down were, and Ceres heard screams and yells of surprise as they fell through the air. She heard sickening crunches as some of them hit posts or the far wall. Several didn't rise, while more screamed with broken limbs. The ones who fell into knots of other prisoners weren't much better off. Ceres heard the fights starting, and clung harder to the chain.

She just had time to wonder what kind of storm could come out of nowhere like this before the boat righted, then swung the other way. Now prisoners crashed into the wall near her, and Ceres curled around Eike, shielding her from the worst of it. For once, Ceres was glad that they'd left her armor on her when they'd thrown her in here. A crazed-looking man landed next to them and lashed out reflexively with a knife that looked like it had been made from a length of bone. It skittered off the steel, and Ceres kicked out, knocking him away.

The ship leveled out once more, but only briefly. Something slammed into the side of the ship, and for a moment, Ceres thought that they must have hit a rock. Then the side of the ship split, and a tentacle as wide as a man was tall burst through.

It seemed they weren't in a storm after all.

"Sea monster!" one of the prisoners screamed, and Ceres heard other voices join in the call.

The tentacle lashed like a whip among the prisoners, wrapping around a pair of men before jerking back. They were chained in place, but the strength of the tentacle was enough to snap them clear of it. Ceres saw one of the prisoners try to cling to the side of the hole in the ship, but the tentacle wrenched him out into the ocean.

Water shot through in a gout that swept people away, seeming to Ceres to pour in impossibly fast. She saw another tentacle punch through the wood of the hold, and then a beak like that of some giant bird of prey followed, tearing its way inside. Water followed each time, and Ceres looked down to find that it was already up to her ankles.

"We're going to sink," she said. "We need to get out of here!"

"How?" Eike asked.

Ceres didn't have an answer for that, but she still headed toward the hatch that led up to the deck. It was covered in wide iron bars, locked firmly from the outside.

"I think I can fit!" Eike said.

"Then go," Ceres replied. "You need to get off the ship!"

She might not be able to save herself, but at least she could save the girl. Other prisoners pushed up behind Ceres, crushing her against the hatch as they tried to get through, but Ceres held them back while Eike wriggled through. She scampered away and Ceres looked back at the hold.

The water was rising now. She could see those prisoners whose shackles held them to a particular spot yanking at them, trying to pull them away from their moorings. One man who had been knocked unconscious by the fall across the hold slid under the water as Ceres watched, while the tentacles of the monster continued to flail inside the hold, dragging helpless prisoners toward that waiting maw. There was nowhere to run to, and already the ship felt as though it was delicately poised, ready to tip over at any moment.

"Quick, Ceres! Up here!"

Ceres looked up and saw sunlight, unencumbered by bars. Eike was there beyond the hatch, a set of keys held proudly in one hand.

"I stole them from a guard," Eike said. "I bet one will open your shackles too!"

She grinned down at Ceres, and Ceres found herself smiling back up. She hauled herself up through the hatch, onto the deck, trying to make sense of what was going on as she took the keys from Eike and fitted them to her shackles. She hurried as much as she could. It wasn't just the rising water. Other prisoners were already pushing their way up onto the deck behind Ceres, and Ceres didn't want to have to fight them for the keys.

The ship was clearly in trouble. The monster attacking it had tentacles wrapped around the masts, tearing men from the rigging and crushing them in its grasp. Ceres saw one sweep around like a flail, knocking sailors and guards into the water like toys. Above, she saw sea raptors gathering, as though sensing the potential feast to come. She saw some of the guards jabbing at the tentacles with swords and harpoons. None of it seemed to make any difference.

She saw one of the guards look over in her direction as she succeeded in getting the shackles off.

"The prisoners are escaping!" he cried, and ran at her with a sword outstretched.

Ceres didn't have any time to think, and the terror of the monster was too great for any more fear to break through. Instead, she swung the shackles that had just confined her around as a weapon, catching the guard on the side of his head and knocking him sprawling. A questing tentacle reached out and grabbed him, dragging him screaming into the water.

More guards came her way, despite the greater threat of the monster attacking them all. Ceres tossed her keys to the prisoners coming through the hatch behind her, then struck out with her shackles at the sword a guard held, tangling it. She moved in close to rip the sword from his grasp, then kicked the guard away.

"You really were a combatlord, weren't you?" Eike said. Despite everything, she sounded surprised by it.

Ceres nodded. "Stay close to me. We have to find a way off this ship."

The ship creaked as if in response to that as the tentacled monster continued to tear through it. One of the masts shivered and fell under the power of its assault, crashing down into the water like some huge tree while Ceres held Eike and tried to keep her back from the danger. There had to be small boats for landing, didn't there? There had to be a way off the ship besides the gangplank.

Ceres barely had a chance to think that before the ship tilted, its bow plunging into the water. The world seemed to turn on its side, and for a moment, she had a view of the water below, filled with blood, struggling men, and the seething mass of the creature attacking them. She could see fins too, as sharks swam around the edges of it, looking to pick up stragglers.

Ceres had a moment to experience the full horror of it before the water came up to meet her. She clung to Eike, but the girl was ripped from her grasp as they plunged into the cold of the sea. Ceres tried to take a breath, tasted salt water, and managed to get her head above the surface for a second.

It didn't last. The weight of her armor dragged her down, and Ceres found herself dropping beneath the waves once more. She fumbled for the straps of her breastplate and iron kilt, swimming free in just her tunic and watching them tumble into the depths among the flailing tentacles and dying prisoners. She saw a whole chain of prisoners dragged down into the depths by their bonds, sharks already plunging in toward them.

She spotted Eike more by chance than anything. A tentacle had wrapped around the girl's leg, ignoring her futile efforts to kick free. Ceres dove down toward Eike, reaching out for the tentacle even though she knew there was no way she could hope to pull it clear. She silently begged for the strength to save the girl, bracing her legs as she tried to break the monster's grip.

Ceres felt the moment when the power that she'd wielded in the Stade come to her like a wave rising within her. It seemed to start somewhere deep inside her, bursting up through her and out into the tentacle that gripped Eike. The power blasted into it and the tentacle let go of the girl, jerking back the way Ceres might have from a hot piece of iron. Ceres grabbed Eike and swam upwards while her lungs burned with the effort.

They broke the surface together, not far from the upturned remains of one of the ship's boats. The rest of it was sinking rapidly, while sailors screamed in the water as they fought sharks, tentacles, or both.

"Quick," Ceres said, "get aboard."

She helped Eike out of the water, then climbed up beside her. A tentacle stretched out toward them, then pulled back, as though some part of the monster could remember what had happened the last time it had touched Ceres. Instead, it grabbed for another of the guards in the water, and the sharks followed close behind.

The feeding frenzy seemed to go on forever, while Ceres sat in the middle of it all on the hull of the small boat, her arms wrapped around Eike for protection. Nothing came close to them. Nothing seemed to dare. Even the sharks that brushed by veered away, making for other prey.

Eventually, the last tentacle plunged back into the water, and stillness replaced the violence that had come before. Ceres looked around for other survivors, but she couldn't see any. The remains of the ship had long since fallen below the water, and anyone clinging to the wreckage had been ruthlessly picked off by tentacles or sharks. Only a spread of splintered wood and supplies showed that the ship had ever been there at all.

"They're dead," Eike said in a small voice. "They're all dead."

Ceres held onto her while the girl started to cry, trying to think of a way to comfort her, even though she could barely find a way past the horror of it herself. "It's all right. I'm here. You're alive, and I'm alive. We'll find a way through this."

Yet as they drifted on the open sea, without any idea where they were, Ceres had no idea how survival would be possible.

CHAPTER TWENTY TWO

Anka kept her head down, trying not to attract attention from the soldiers of the 23rd as she walked through the city of tents. So far, she'd been lucky. She'd had nothing more than a few suspicious looks. With the way soldiers were, it could be a lot worse.

She'd managed to gain entry to the camp by dressing as one of the washer women who made their way between the campfires. There were no female soldiers in the army but there were always servants and camp followers who trailed after it as it moved. Dressed as one of them, she was as invisible as if she'd crept in under the cover of darkness.

At least, she hoped so.

She didn't want to think about what might happen to her if they caught her, or worse, what might happen to the rebellion. Since Rexus had died, she'd been the one trying to pull things together, assuring people that they could still continue, and still succeed. She'd smoothed over arguments, passed messages, and found ways to persuade their supporters that it wouldn't rebound on them.

Every second she spent away from Delos cost the rebellion dearly, but she kept picking her way through the camp, holding her bundle of washing like a protective shield. Whatever it cost, she'd promised Ceres that she would do this.

That mattered to her, more than enough for her to brave the stares and occasional catcalls of the soldiers as she passed, and to dodge past the larger groups of them. Ceres had given her back her freedom. Without her, Anka would be suffering a lot worse than this.

The hard part was finding one conscript in the middle of the Empire's vast army. Sympathizers had provided some information, bribery had gotten her more, but ultimately, Anka had found herself having to track along the route the conscript takers had followed, asking questions and hoping for the best.

She knew that wouldn't work here. Ask after Sartes, and it would bring as much trouble for him as for her. Anka looked around the army camp, trying to make sense of where she was. In the distance, she could see soldiers drilling in lines and running while officers shouted at them. Others dug ditches or cut wood for palisades.

She passed by a space between the tents where a soldier was tied to a post, being whipped for some infraction. She could hear the muffled cries as the man bit down on a leather strap to keep from screaming, while other soldiers, probably members of his unit, stood around to watch the punishment.

Anka didn't stay for it. Hating the army wasn't the same thing as wanting to see the individuals in it hurt. Instead, she headed for the larger tents near the center of the camp. The army had to keep records somewhere, didn't it? Surely there would be payrolls, or details of who served with whom? A roll call or a note of punishments dished out? Something, at least.

In her disguise, she was able to get closer to the tents than she would have believed. No one challenged her. Probably it helped that she walked briskly, trying to look as though she knew where she was going, while looking around out of the corner of her eye until she was sure that she did.

She found the tent she was looking for next to a larger commander's pavilion, and slipped in once she was sure that no one was looking. It made sense that the 23rd's commanders would want to keep their adjutants and administrators close by. Sure enough, a writing slope and parchment sat on a folding camp table, along with box after box that clearly held records.

Anka dared a glance outside before she began, wanting to make sure that no one found her. This was the most dangerous part, because no one but a spy would ever go through the army's papers. She pressed down the anxiety and started work.

Anka went as quickly as she could. She took out records, trying to make sense of the crabbed writing there as she scanned them for any glimpse of Sartes's name. If she could get some sense of where he was in the camp, that would be the best possible outcome, but even confirmation that he was really here and still alive would be enough.

She froze as she heard the sound of footsteps outside the tent, then quickly shoved the rolls back into place. She finished, grabbed her bundle of washing, and just about made it to the door when an officer walked in.

"Watch where you're going!" the officer bellowed, then paused. His hand shot out to grip Anka's shoulder. "Wait, what are you even doing here? Old Mersha handles my washing."

Anka didn't have to feign the shudder that ran through her. "I don't know, my lord. She sent me out, and I… I thought this was where I was meant to be." She grabbed for one of the names she'd seen on the papers she'd looked through. "I was looking for Captain Thero's tent?"

"Well, you're on the wrong side of the camp, then," the officer said. "He keeps his tent in the north quadrant. Don't you know anything?"

"I... I'm new, my lord," Anka said. Again, she didn't have to fake the fear. If this man guessed what she was really doing there, she would never leave the camp. "The north quadrant, you say?"

The officer waved a hand. "*That* way, you stupid girl. Now hurry. Captain Thero isn't a man to keep waiting."

Anka hurried from the tent with what she hoped was the right level of gratitude, setting off in the direction the officer had indicated but then quickly veering off in case he worked out that she wasn't all she seemed. She took deep breaths as she tried to think.

She hadn't gotten anything from the records. Sartes's name hadn't been anywhere in the ones she'd looked through, and there seemed to be no obvious way to find him without that kind of clue where he might be. Anka didn't even know for sure if he was in this camp. Everything she'd gotten from her contacts had been supposition and fragments.

The truth was that no one kept track of where individual conscripts went. The army didn't care about them enough for that, and just that fact was enough to make Anka angry. What kind of world did they live in where no one cared what happened to one boy, because he would probably be dead soon anyway?

Even if she hadn't promised Ceres to find her brother, that would have been enough to make Anka keep going. How *long* could she keep going though? she wondered. Could she really justify looking for one boy forever when the rebellion could save many more young men and women? She didn't even really know what Sartes looked like.

That thought brought despair with it, and Anka started to make her way through the tents toward the edge of the encampment. Anka had tried to tell herself that this was an easier task than trying to overthrow a whole empire, but the truth was that it was almost impossible.

In spite of her promise to Ceres, she couldn't stop herself from thinking about going home then. The rebellion needed her, and if she couldn't find Sartes here, then all she could do was get herself captured or killed. The thought of having to give up ate at her, but Anka couldn't think what else she could do. To put off the moment when she would have to make a decision, she circled back toward the command tents. Perhaps she would be able to make one more attempt to look through the army's records, although if they caught her this time...

She waited by the pavilions and marquees belonging to the army's officers, staying in the shadows and looking for an opportunity to sneak inside. She waited, trying to make it look as though she was working on something in her bundle of washing, and that was when she heard the name she'd been hoping for since she got there.

"Sergeant, I have messages I need carrying across camp. What happened to that conscript of yours?"

Anka peeked around the tent to see an officer in gilded armor talking with a burly man who was obviously of a lower rank.

"Sartes, sir?"

"How should I remember the boy's name? The one who has been so useful. Just get him."

"Yes sir."

Anka watched the whole exchange with her heart in her mouth. When the sergeant set off, she followed him, using all the caution she'd learned in Delos. It was safer doing this than waiting around the command tents, because at least she could pretend to be on an errand again.

She followed until the sergeant reached a training ring where conscripts were working on their swordplay. Already, two had deep-looking wounds, because the sharp weapons they were using had no room for mistakes. She saw the sergeant pause on the edge of the training ring.

"Sartes! Get yourself out here!"

Anka looked at the boy who disengaged himself from the melee. He had sandy hair and a wiry frame made thinner by the harshness of the army. At first glance, it was hard to see the resemblance between him and Ceres, yet there was a hint of similarity there, and this was definitely him.

"The officers have work for you, boy," the sergeant said. "Get over to the commander's tent before they have you whipped!"

Anka saw the boy take off at a dead run. She hated to see that fear there, but another emotion rose beside it: hope. She'd done what she promised. She'd found Sartes.

But now she needed to find a way to save him—before the army killed him.

CHAPTER TWENTY THREE

If they kept drifting out to sea like this, Ceres felt, they would die. Ceres was certain of it. Either the sun would bake them, or predators would come for them, realizing that Ceres no longer had the strength to fight them off.

The small boat had a piece of driftwood they could use as a makeshift paddle, but there seemed to be nowhere to paddle to. Instead, they bobbed along like some child's toy, at the mercy of the wind and the currents.

Ceres's lips cracked with thirst as they floated. She barely had the strength to lift her head and look out over the expanse of the water that stretched to the horizon in every direction.

She heard Eike moan beside her. The girl was barely conscious now, because despite the water all around them, there was none that they could risk drinking. Eike hadn't believed Ceres when she'd warned her about it, and had quickly thrown up the salt water. Ceres shook her, and her eyes barely flickered open.

Ceres looked around again, seeing the seabirds above that followed them, obviously waiting for the moment when they would finally succumb. One came close, and Ceres waved it away.

That was when she saw the island.

It appeared as a speck on the horizon at first, small enough that Ceres wasn't even certain that it was there.

As the currents carried their boat toward it though, she saw the sandy beaches and rocky rises there, leading to what looked like jungles on the interior.

And for the first time, her heart filled with hope.

*

Ceres paddled for shore with their rough wooden oar for what felt like hours. She ignored the way her muscles protested at the sudden effort after drifting for so long, keeping going until they were passing by tooth-like rocks, then on into the breakers leading to a beach.

Ceres leapt out, pulling the boat up onto the sand with Eike still in it. She lifted the girl up, helping her out and then supporting her as they set off along the beach in search of fresh water.

She didn't know what was going to happen next. She wasn't sure where they were, or what would happen to them in the next few days. She wasn't sure if she would ever see home again, and that thought was a frightening one. Right then, Ceres was just grateful to be alive.

Ceres felt the eyes on her long before anyone stepped out of the surrounding jungle. She watched the fronds near the edge, seeing some rustle in a way that might have just been the wind.

People emerged, dressed in plain tunics and dresses, supplemented by what looked like leaves and branches from the forest. Some seemed to have flowers tangled in their hair, while others wore vines wrapped around them like jewelry.

Ceres stood there cautiously. She wasn't sure how these people would react to strangers, or what was going to happen next.

It was only as they got closer that Ceres saw they weren't wearing costumes after all. Instead, she saw vines and twigs emerging from flesh, skin that had given way to the roughness of bark or the green of leaves.

Two came forward with bowls of water, and Ceres took one gratefully, before helping Eike to sip at hers. The girl seemed to regain some strength with the liquid, rousing enough to look around. Ceres saw her start at the sight of the people around them.

"What are they?" Eike asked.

"We are the folk of the forest," a voice said, and Ceres saw a man step forward from the crowd of people. "Welcome."

He was tall and slender, probably only a few years older than Ceres was, with skin that seemed to vary between delicately tanned and mossy green where it wasn't covered by a tunic. He wasn't broad across the shoulders, but Ceres could see the muscles that stood out as he moved. He had strong features, with high cheekbones and a smile that seemed to come easily. His hair was dark, cut through here and there with a tangle of flowering vines, while his eyes were such a vibrant green that Ceres couldn't bring herself to look away from him.

He seemed to be looking back at her with the same intensity.

"I'm Ceres," she said.

"I am Eoin," he replied.

"You're in charge here?" Ceres asked.

Eoin smiled. "People sometimes listen to me, but the truth is that all of us with the sickness follow the way of the forest."

"Sickness?" Ceres heard Eike ask. "You're sick?"

Eoin spread his hands. "They call it a sickness, or a curse. They send us here because they don't want us around them. We live out our time here, until the forest claims us. But you don't have to worry."

He held out a hand to Eike, and to Ceres's surprise, the girl took it.

"We'll go back to the village and talk more there," he said. Ceres saw him look over to her again. "I think there is a lot to talk about. The ocean has brought you to us for a reason."

They set off in the direction of the jungle, and Ceres followed Eoin along a trail where the trees arched over them as though forming a tunnel. She glanced up and saw a bird flit from one branch to another, and impossibly, it seemed to glow with golden light as it did so. She turned to point it out to Eike, but the girl was already staring at another part of the forest.

Ceres followed her gaze and froze in place. A horse of the purest white stood there, a horn of gold jutting from its forehead as it reared up. Ceres's breath caught at the sight. A unicorn? But they were only meant to be myths.

Eoin seemed to understand her amazement. "The creatures of magic still have places where they gather," he said. "The jungle is one of them. It isn't far now to the settlement."

They kept going, and Ceres saw the jungle open out. There were houses there, but it took her a moment to realize that they were houses, because they seemed more like giant plants, grown into their shapes rather than constructed. She saw huts and treehouses, buildings that were more like simple platforms in the branches. The only stone building she could see was a kind of ziggurat at the center of it all, and that looked as though it might have been there long before the rest of it.

There were plants there, and animals that seemed impossible. A lizard flew past Ceres's head on butterfly wings, while further over, she saw a beetle the size of a small dog. She saw trees too, warped and twisted until they almost seemed like strange sculptures of people.

"Those are the ones the curse has claimed," Eoin said.

"You mean those are *people*?" Eike said. Ceres could hear the horror in her voice. She could feel some of it herself.

"They were," Eoin said. "Eventually, the curse takes all of us, and we go back to the forest. It can't be stopped. All we can do is live our lives until then."

"That's terrible," Ceres said.

Eoin shrugged. "It is not so bad. It is beautiful here, and we have enough."

He led the way to a hut, where there was food waiting: fruit and tubers taken from the jungle. Ceres and Eike ate hungrily, while Eoin and the others joined them.

"How did you come to be here?" Eoin asked.

"It's a long story," Ceres said.

Eoin smiled. "There should always be time for stories, and we would like to hear."

Ceres did her best to explain it. She told them about what was happening in the Empire, and how she'd come to fight in the Stade. She told them about her last fight, and how she'd ended up condemned to the Isle of Prisoners.

All the while, Eoin's eyes stayed on her. It felt as though he could see right through her, looking past the surface to something else underneath. Ceres wasn't sure what it was that he could see, but right then, she'd never felt that vulnerable with anyone.

"You're a warrior?" he asked. "Perhaps that explains some of why you were sent to us."

"What do you mean?" Ceres asked.

Eoin stood, offering his hand. "Come with me. I promise that your friend will be safe here."

Ceres believed him. She'd never seen anywhere that seemed as peaceful as this hidden village. It just seemed natural to reach out and take his hand, feeling the strength there.

She let him lead her out and through the village, to a space on the far side of the ziggurat that had been cleared in a wide circle. There, she could see two young women fighting, surrounded by a small knot of villagers.

The two held no weapons, but they didn't seem to need them. Ceres could barely keep up as they blurred and spun, their hands and feet lashing out from every angle. They dodged and leapt, then came together as they tried to lock one another's limbs and throw each other to the ground. When they tumbled there together, they kept fighting, until Ceres saw one slip behind the other as quickly as a snake, her arm locking around her opponent's throat. The two got up, laughing, and began again.

It was like the training she'd done for the Stade, and yet totally unlike it. The fighting there had been brutal and efficient, while there was something beautiful about this, something that seemed to Ceres to be perfectly in balance.

"It's amazing," she said. "To be able to fight that well without weapons."

"They simply move in harmony with the world," Eoin replied. "As for weapons, we have them, but we have little need for them."

He reached around to his back, producing a dagger that seemed to be made from dark, glassy stone. He passed it to her. Ceres tested the edge, and to her surprise, it was as sharp as any steel.

"For you," he said. "You have been sent here for a reason, Ceres. I'm sure of that. I don't know what that reason is, but we will teach you what we can of our ways. If you want, that is."

Her answer was obvious.

"I want to."

CHAPTER TWENTY FOUR

As he went down to the castle's gardens, Thanos found himself looking around suspiciously. The pressure of what he was doing weighed down on him now, and he found himself looking for a spot where he could just be himself for a moment without risking his life.

Everywhere else in the castle, it seemed that he had to hide what he felt and who he was. If anyone saw his anger over what had happened to Ceres, if anyone saw through the act he'd put up to his sympathies for the rebels, then he would be dead, noble of the Empire or not.

They would call him a traitor, when the truth was that they were the ones betraying the interests of their own people. They were the ones taking from their people, and Thanos had heard how much worse it had gotten since he'd left. He'd heard about the parties under Lucious's command, ravaging the countryside. Just the thought of it made him grit his teeth in anger.

He needed to find a way to stay calm, so he stood out there and looked at the blooms, imagining how Ceres might react if she were here. Would she appreciate the gentle beauty of the flowers, or would she want to be in the training pits for the Stade? Thanos smiled at the fact that he had an easier time imagining her there than here.

The smile faded as he thought about what was happening to her now. He had to find a way to help her if he could, but Thanos wasn't sure what he could do to stop Ceres being taken to the Isle of Prisoners. He couldn't just overturn the king's decision, and if he tried, he would immediately be suspect. He could try to get a message to the rebellion, perhaps, but-

"I'm not interrupting you, am I?"

Thanos turned to see Stephania approaching. She looked lovely in the night air, but then, she always looked lovely. She seemed to hesitate for a moment, then threw her arms around him, hugging him tightly. The suddenness of it caught Thanos a little by surprise, and so did the action itself. He'd always thought Stephania was too proper and reserved for such a show of emotion.

"I'm so glad that you're safe," Stephania said as she stepped back. "When I heard that you'd been killed…"

Thanos heard the catch there in her voice, and saw the faint gleam in her eyes that suggested she might be trying to hold back tears.

"It's all right," he said, reaching out to touch her arm as he tried to comfort her.

"It is now," Stephania said. "Because you're alive. Did you really survive because some fishermen found you?"

Thanos nodded. Even with Stephania, he couldn't afford to tell the truth. Maybe especially with Stephania, because it would never occur to her to keep from saying what she knew around the court. She'd always been the heart of the gossip there.

Bizarrely though, it felt wrong to be deceiving her like this.

"The fishermen saved me," Thanos said. It was true, as far as it went. Without the two men who'd found him, he would never have met Akila's rebels. "They brought me back."

"Then we all owe them a great deal," Stephania said. Thanos saw her half close her eyes. "*I* owe them a great deal. Are they still in Delos?"

Thanos shook his head. "I think they sailed back to Haylon."

"That's a pity," Stephania said. "I would have liked to reward them for bringing you back safely. Someone *really* sent the Typhoon as an assassin?"

She sounded to Thanos as though she couldn't quite believe it even now. Maybe she didn't want to believe it. Stephania was in that side of the court that was nearly oblivious to what was going on outside, not cruel the way some could be, but so self-absorbed that it seemed as though the harsh things out in the world weren't really happening.

Thanos nodded. "He stabbed me in the back on the beach. I think the idea was that it would look as though I'd been killed in the assault."

Stephania nodded. "That was what they told us here. They told us that you were the first out onto the beach, cut down by the rebels. They wanted to make us think you'd died some heroic death."

"You didn't think I could manage a heroic death?" Thanos asked, but the joke did nothing to lighten the mood.

"When I heard it, it felt as though the whole world was collapsing in on me." She looked up at him, and Thanos could see the way her breathing quickened. "Can I... can I see what they did to you? It doesn't seem real somehow without that."

Thanos only hesitated a moment before lifting his tunic to let her see. It wasn't the kind of request he would have expected from someone as proper as Stephania, but he could hear the concern there in her voice.

He saw her reach out carefully, even tenderly, to touch the spot where Akila's men had stitched him back together. He winced reflexively.

"Sorry," Stephania said. "Does it still hurt?"

"A little," Thanos said.

She paused. "You said before that you don't know who sent the Typhoon to assassinate you. Is that true, or were you just holding back so they wouldn't hear you?"

It caught Thanos a little by surprise that she would realize he might do that. It was easy to forget sometimes that Stephania had grown up in the games of the court, and that even her great beauty hadn't kept her out of them. If anything, it had probably made her a target for the jealousy of some of the others there.

"I really don't know," he admitted. "I plan to find out, though."

He saw Stephania nod at that. She seemed to consider for a moment. "I want to help you."

Thanos stared at her in surprise. "You do?"

"Of course I do," Stephania said. "It was when I thought you were gone. Seeing how close you came to dying like this... I want to find who did this to you, and I want them to pay for it."

Thanos could hear the determination there, fierce and hard behind Stephania's otherwise gentle exterior. He hadn't realized that she cared about him that much. He'd always assumed that the promise of marriage to him was purely political for her.

"I swear to you," Stephania said. "I will help you to find the person who gave the order for you to be killed."

Thanos reached out to touch her face. "You've always been so good to me," he said. "Better than I deserve."

Stephania shook her head. "That doesn't matter. You were only doing what the king and queen made you do. What matters is that you're here. You're alive, and we're going to find out who tried to do this to you."

Thanos stood back to look at her then; really look at her. It felt as though he'd never truly seen Stephania before that moment. He'd always seen her as one of the silly young women of the court, too caught up in her own luxurious lifestyle to think about anyone else. He'd assumed that she was vain, selfish, and probably only interested in the latest parties. Certainly, on a night like this, he'd have thought she'd be getting ready for the Festival of the Moon rather than seeking him out.

Yet looking at her now, it was as though he could see through all that to a core of steel underneath. She stood there in the garden, and she should have fit in with the elegance of the flowers there, but it was worth remembering how many of those flowers had thorns. It felt better than he could have imagined to have an ally like that in the court.

"I was a fool," Thanos said, shaking his head. "I should never have treated you the way I did."

"It's all right," Stephania assured him. "I understand."

"Forgive me?" Thanos asked.

"There is nothing to forgive. The only question now is how we're going to find whoever sent the assassin after you."

Thanos nodded. It was a relief to hear that from Stephania, and a weight off his conscience that she hadn't been hurt by the way he'd pushed her aside for Ceres.

"I don't know how I'm going to do it," he admitted.

"How *we're* going to do it," Stephania said. Her hand fit into his neatly, seeming so natural there to Thanos. "This isn't something you should have to do by yourself. I want you to tell me everything you find out. I want to know."

"That means a lot," Thanos said. "But we still need somewhere to start."

Stephania was quiet for a long time, and Thanos found himself wondering what she was thinking. There was obviously something that she wanted to say but wasn't. Strange that he should feel close enough to her to know that.

"What is it?" he asked.

"There... might be something," Stephania said. "I was in the stables a while ago, getting ready to go riding, and I heard one of the stable boys boasting that he was a close friend of Lucious, and that he did favors for him that no one else could."

"It sounds like empty boasting," Thanos said.

Stephania nodded. "That's what the other stable hands said at the time, but the boy showed them a dagger that he could never have afforded alone, and he was talking about taking messages to someone in the army."

"The Typhoon?" Thanos guessed.

He saw Stephania shrug. "I don't know. Not for sure. I don't think even Lucious would be stupid enough to tell a stable boy what he was planning. But it was enough to make me think of it. I don't know if it's anything, though."

Thanos put his hands on Stephania's shoulders. "Thank you for this. It's more than you think."

It was a start, at least. And if the trail did lead back to Lucious...well... then Thanos would make sure that it was an end for the prince as well.

CHAPTER TWENTY FIVE

Ceres gasped for breath as water thundered down onto her. The waterfall hammered into her and she reeled with it, having to fight to keep going. She had no idea why Eoin thought that directly under one was the right place to train in the combat arts they used on the island, but right now she wished that he'd picked somewhere, anywhere, else.

Eoin, of course, stood in the shallow pool beneath it as calmly as if he were in summer rain. He barely even seemed to lift his voice to be heard above it. "This is called Clouds Weaving."

Ceres shook with the effort as she tried to copy the movements Eoin made. She tried to concentrate in spite of the relentless battering of the water, but it was almost impossible to get every detail correct, and Eoin seemed to want perfection in every motion. It seemed to be the one area where his ready smile disappeared as he made her repeat the movements over and over.

She saw him weave through it again: a complex back and forth movement of his hands that looked more like the kind of thing a dancer in the city might have done than anything to do with fighting. She tried to copy the movement and Eoin shook his head.

"Slower."

That was the hardest part of all this. She was used to the rough and tumble fighting of the Stade, but the islanders' way of fighting seemed to involve what looked to Ceres like slow motion dancing. She wanted to speed up, to *fight*.

"When can we go faster?" Ceres asked.

"When you can do it right slowly," Eoin said. He finally smiled. "You're making progress, but you have to learn to move in harmony with the world, Ceres. Learn the lessons it has to teach you."

"And what lesson does standing in a waterfall teach me?" Ceres asked, as the water continued to beat down on her.

She saw Eoin's hands flow through the movement again. "I don't know. People learn their own lessons. Maybe it will be that the softest things can become hard and relentless. Maybe it will be to let the world flow off you smoothly." His smile widened. "Perhaps that if you're going to get wet anyway, you might as well embrace it."

Ceres wanted to argue with that, and with the endless training that seemed to have so little to do with fighting. Before she could do it though, one of the other forest people ran up to them. This one was further along in the disease than Eoin was, almost as much plant as human.

"Eoin, we have people landing on the slate shore. It looks like raiders heading for the village."

Ceres heard Eoin sigh. "Will they never learn? All right, I'll come."

"Should I stay here with Ceres?" the newcomer asked.

"I should come," Ceres said. "Maybe I can help."

Eoin waved a hand in dismissal. "We can handle it. But perhaps you can learn something by watching. Follow me."

He ran along the trails that led through the jungle toward the village, and Ceres had a hard time keeping up. She was strong and fast, but Eoin seemed to flit through the trees as naturally as if he were a part of them. By the time they reached the edge of the village, Ceres was out of breath, while Eoin looked as though he could have run for another hour.

She could see men running through the village, weapons in their hands. For a moment, Ceres thought they might be soldiers of the Empire, there to hunt her, and fear ran through her. Then she saw the roughness of their weapons and the piecemeal nature of their armor. These really were pirates and raiders, not the army.

That didn't make their intentions any better. As she watched, one of the raiders rushed into a low hut, and there was a scream from within. On the edge of the jungle, Ceres looked over to Eoin.

"What do we do now?" Ceres asked.

Eoin pointed to a spot. "You wait here."

"But I can fight," she insisted. She didn't want to stand by while other people risked their lives.

Eoin shook his head. "Not yet, but you *will* be able to. For now, watch. Learn."

Ceres didn't want to hold back like that, but as she started to take a step forward, she felt the firm hand of one of the forest people on her shoulder. She stood there because there seemed to be no other choice, and she watched as Eoin ran into the village.

The forest people joined him as he ran, seeming to come from nowhere as they stepped out of hidden spots in the trees and bushes. With their curse, they blended in perfectly. They reminded Ceres of the water from the waterfall as they plunged down among the houses they were trying to defend, washing over the landing party of raiders.

In the instant before they struck, Ceres had to admit to a moment of fear. The raiders were heavily armed, strong looking and clearly dangerous. Some of the forest folk, by contrast, seemed too delicate and frond-like to do any real damage.

The moment the fight started though, it became clear that she needn't have worried. Despite their lack of weapons, the islanders moved with a deadly kind of grace, never quite there as their opponents attacked, striking back with blows that seemed languid, but which felled the raiders wherever they struck.

Ceres watched Eoin at the heart of it, and he moved like water. He swayed aside from the sweep of an ax, then brought his forearm around in a blow to the collarbone of his assailant that sent the man to his knees. He brought up his foot in a kick that seemed to be all grace and elegance until it snapped the raider's head back.

Ceres saw a swordsman move in close to Eoin and she tried to call out a warning, but she was too far away for him to ever hear it.

He didn't need the warning though. He turned instead, and his eyes seemed to fix on Ceres for an instant. Then his hands moved in a pattern that was far too familiar, because Ceres had been practicing it all morning. Eoin waved his way through the delicate movements of Weaving Clouds, and somewhere in it he twisted the sword out of his attacker's hands. The blow that he answered with only seemed to touch the raider, but the man dropped like a stone.

It took the islanders a matter of minutes to kill their attackers, and they *did* kill them. There was something unstoppably ruthless about the way they moved through the raiders, leaving none alive, letting none run back to their boats. When they were done, they carried the bodies into the jungle as gently as if they were carrying respected friends.

All Ceres could do was stand there in something close to amazement. Unarmed, sick as they were, they'd defeated a whole landing party of armed men.

Maybe there was plenty to learn here after all.

***

That night, Ceres sat at one of the fires in the village, eating the fruits of the forest while above the stars seemed to swirl as clouds passed. Eike was there beside her, while Eoin and several of the other villagers sat there too.

Eoin played a many-stringed instrument that seemed to respond to the least touch, music floating through the night air as he tapped the notes. It was so peaceful that Ceres might almost have been able to dismiss the attack earlier as a bad dream if she hadn't seen it herself.

"Do people often attack your island?" Ceres asked. She couldn't just ignore what had happened today.

"Sometimes," Eoin said. "They think that because we are cursed, we are weak. It is less common than it was. They used to raid regularly before we learned to fight back."

"How did you all get so good at fighting?" Ceres asked.

"We watched the world," Eoin said. "We learned the lessons of the forest. But we should talk of happier things. The moment for fighting has passed. You could tell us about your lives."

Ceres shook her head. "There isn't much that's happy to tell there. My father left. My mother sold me as a slave. The people I care about most are dead."

"The past can be hard," Eoin agreed. "My family cast me out when they realized I was one of the forest folk. Most of those here have a similar story."

There were nods from around the fire.

"But the future can be different," Eoin said. "Tell us about your hopes and your dreams."

Ceres tried to think. "Once, I dreamed that I would be a famous combatlord, fighting in the Stade. I guess I've already achieved that dream. Then I dreamed that maybe there could be something else for me with the man who…" She shook her head. "It doesn't matter. He died."

She heard the notes from Eoin's instrument still as he reached out to touch her hand. "I'm sorry. What now though?"

Ceres thought for a moment.

"Now," Ceres said, "there are a lot of things I want. I have a brother, and I want him to be safe. I want to get back to my father, and make sure he's found Sartes." She tightened her hands in anger. "I want revenge on the people who tried to kill me. But after that… I guess I want to change things if I can. I want to make a better world."

Eoin laughed gently. "A better world would be nice. What about you, little one? What do you dream?"

Eike looked a little surprised to be included, to Ceres's eyes.

"I don't know," she admitted, hugging her knees. "I guess I just want somewhere I'll be safe, and fit in."

"I think that might be easy enough," Eoin said, with a sweep of his arm that took in the camp. People were dancing and singing around their fires now, and Ceres could feel the pulse of it running through her. Even so, she didn't join in.

"What about you?" Ceres asked. "What do you want for the future?"

"The future is tricky for us," Eoin said, gesturing around at the island. "We know that eventually, the forest will claim us. We know that the world does not want us. We have learned to live *now,* and see what we can leave behind." He gestured to some of the others. "Jan here has his pottery. K'sala is trying to weave the perfect tapestry. Many of us try to understand the world as much as we can, or seek happiness with one another."

"And you?" Ceres asked, not willing to let it go.

"I have my music," Eoin said. "And I have the safety of the people here to think about. I want to make sure this remains a community where any of us can feel safe and happy. Those are probably dreams that are big enough for one life, don't you think?"

Ceres found herself hoping that he might say more than that. "What about building a life with someone?" she asked. "What about love?"

She saw Eoin look away.

"Love would just mean someone left behind when the forest finally took me," he said.

"But it might also mean being happy until then," Ceres pointed out. She looked into the fire, watching it dance. "Maybe that's worth it."

"Maybe," Eoin agreed. "For now though, we should all get some sleep. If you want to achieve *your* dreams, Ceres, you still have a lot of training to do."

That was true, and in that moment determination filled Ceres. She had seen what the islanders could do. She was going to learn what they had to teach. She was going to return to Delos, and she was going to change things.

Whatever it took.

CHAPTER TWENTY SIX

Sartes had a plan. He reminded himself of that over and over as he started to make his way across the 23rd's camp, slipping through the early evening activity of the place like a stranger. He had a plan for his escape. Now, he had to hope that it would work.

Repeating it should have made him feel better, but instead, it just reminded him of how big the stakes were. The punishment for a conscript trying to escape was death, without exception. The best-case scenario would be a quick sword thrust as he tried to get clear of the camp. The worst... they might make his fellow conscripts do it, beating Sartes to death to prove their loyalty. He had no doubt that they would do it. They would be too frightened to do anything else.

In some ways, Sartes's plan was simple: he was going to walk to the edge of the camp, then make his way through the stakes and trip wires, pits and cordons that surrounded it. The complex part was actually doing it.

The fact that he'd managed to become useful to the officers around the camp helped. It had gotten people used to the idea that he could move around the camp, when most of the conscripts were carefully controlled. It had let him work out the timing of the guard changes and the locations of the worst traps around the camp.

"I can do this," Sartes told himself as he kept moving among the tents.

"Do what, conscript?" an officer demanded, stepping into his path. Sartes recognized him as one of the training masters. Varion, Sartes thought his name was.

"Deliver this message, sir," Sartes said, pulling out one of half a dozen he had hidden away. "The captain said it was urgent."

The training master read it through, looked at the seal on the bottom, and then shoved it back at Sartes.

"All right, get on with it, conscript."

Sartes hurried off, and he was glad right then that he'd picked one of the real messages, given the way the officer had checked the seal. He'd carefully collected messages before he'd set out, going round to as many officers as he could to gather them, because the more messages he had to deliver, the more access he had to the rest of the camp.

He'd forged more, scribbling messages on whatever parchment he could steal from the quartermaster's stores. He couldn't fight his way out of the camp, but his stock of messages and orders would let him use the machinery of the army itself as a kind of protection.

Even so, he had to hurry. There was no message or errand that would get a conscript out of the camp without at least a dozen real soldiers there to accompany him. That meant Sartes had to sneak out in one of the small windows between guard changes, when things were confused. Miss that window, and the whole escape attempt would be for nothing.

Miss that window, and he would never reach the rebellion. He might never see his family again. He would never see his sister, and the thought of that was enough to make a knot form in Sartes's stomach.

So he hurried through the camp, brandishing his sheaf of orders like a shield. He was almost to the edge when another officer stopped him.

"You, you're the boy who carries messages for the general, aren't you?"

"Yes, sir."

"Well then, I want you to go to his tent and get me the latest maps for our preparations against the rebellion. I've been sent orders, but I have no idea where I'm actually supposed to take my men. Tell them Leus sent you. Here, you'll need this."

The officer handed over a signet ring, standing there in obvious expectation. Sartes saluted, because he couldn't think what else to do. He set off back in the direction of the center of the camp for the same reason, although he veered off into the tents as soon as he could, planning to double back.

He stopped, with his hand on the rough canvas of one of the tents. He held up the signet ring, looking at the worked silver of the design. If he ran now, this might be worth something to the rebellion, giving it the chance to forge orders until the officer admitted what had happened.

But the man had talked about orders for attacks on the rebellion. The maps for that would be worth far more. Yet if he went for the maps and plans, how much time would that take? He'd planned out his escape to the last minute. Any delay, and they might find him.

That thought terrified Sartes more than anything. He couldn't go back now, and if he was caught, it wouldn't be a quick death. He couldn't afford for anything to go wrong when he'd planned it all so carefully.

Yet if Sartes ran now, and people died because they didn't know where the attacks would come, he would always feel responsible. He had to at least try to get them. He had enough time, if he sprinted. He hoped.

Sartes ran back toward the command tents, and now he must have looked like what he was: a conscript who had just been given an urgent instruction by a superior and who didn't want to waste a single instant in following it.

He made it to the commander's tent and stood panting in front of the guards for a moment, holding up the officer's ring.

"Leus wants the maps for the next attack," he managed.

"In a hurry, is he?"

"Yes, sir."

"Then you'd better get in there and grab them. The general's observing evening drill, so you'll have to find them yourself."

Sartes could barely believe his luck. He had to force himself to move into the general's tent slowly so that it would look normal to the guards. Only once he was safely inside the pavilion did he start to sort through any papers he could see, trying to work out how much he could get away with taking without the guards realizing what was happening.

In the end, he took as much as he could fit under one arm, wrapping it up in the map he'd been sent for and walking out with as much confidence as he could muster. He half expected the guards to try to stop him then, but neither even seemed to notice.

"Better run, boy," one of them joked. "You don't want to be late."

"You don't know how true that is," Sartes said, and set off across the camp at a run again. Fear pushed him forward, not knowing if he'd already taken too long.

He had his route planned out already. He'd learned his way between the tents, and followed the signs and banners now. He dodged the officers and guards where he could, both because he couldn't afford any more delays and because there was too much chance of them seeing what he was carrying. Now that he'd taken the risk of getting the plans, he couldn't let them go.

He made his way to the spot he'd picked out for his escape. There was a space near one corner of the encampment where the wooden walls gave way to picket lines and there were trees not far away. The guards handed over their watch nearer the middle of the lines, before marching out, so if he'd timed it right—

"You there!" a voice called. "What are you doing there?"

Sartes looked round to see a guard approaching. The man was older than him and larger, in full armor, armed with sword, shield, and spear.

"I asked you a question, boy. What are you doing here?"

"I have orders," Sartes said automatically, but he knew it wouldn't work.

"No conscript leaves. Those are the orders that matter. Deserter!" The guard cupped his hands over his mouth, ready to call it again.

Sartes saw a figure rush out from the tents, then smash into the guard. A hammer rose and fell, once, then again. The guard went down and didn't rise. The figure straightened up, and Sartes stared at him in absolute shock.

"Father?"

He still couldn't believe it, yet it *was* his father. He stood there, looking exactly as Sartes remembered him from the days before he'd left. Sartes threw his arms wide, rushing forward to hug his father on instinct.

"Sartes!"

He felt his father hug him back, and for the first time since he'd arrived in the camp, Sartes had a moment where he felt safe.

"It's so good to see you," his father said. "I thought I'd never find you."

"What are you doing here?" Sartes asked. He shook his head. "It doesn't matter. I'm so glad to see you."

"I came looking for you. Smiths can always find a way into an army camp." His father stood back and looked at him at arm's length. "Are you all right? Have they hurt you?"

"I'm all right," Sartes assured him. "I managed to avoid the worst of it."

"I'm glad," his father said. "Ceres told me I needed to be the one to come and find you before it got worse."

"Ceres?" Sartes said. "Is she here?"

That would have been the best possible outcome. His whole family back together, all at once. The excitement that briefly rose in him sank again as his father shook his head.

"She's fighting in the Stade," his father said. "She said she couldn't run away from that. But we'll get her. We'll go back and find her if we can."

Sartes nodded. "We will, and then it will be better, right?"

"I hope so," his father said. "First though, we need to get you out of here. That shout will bring trouble."

Sartes swallowed at that thought. "I have a way out. Quick, this way."

It felt strange to be the one leading the way for his father, but Sartes was the one who knew his way through the defenses around the camp. He'd worked out his route, and now he forced himself to concentrate on it, avoiding the pits and the stakes that kept conscripts in as much as they kept others out.

"Through here," he said.

"We need to hurry," his father insisted. "What's that you have there? Leave it, we need to run."

Already, Sartes could hear the clamor in the camp. Horns sounded an alarm, and he could see soldiers running about as they tried to work out what was happening.

"I can't. I have plans showing what the Empire plans against the rebellion."

"What?" His father was the one standing there in shock now. "I'd ask how you managed that, but I don't think there's any time. They'll be coming. We need to go."

Sartes's heart felt like it was in his mouth. This wasn't how he'd planned on this. His whole escape plan had been about slipping away quietly, and being well away by the time anyone noticed. He'd figured that no one would follow if it was too much trouble.

Now, though, he could hear the sounds of hunting parties being formed. Horns sounded, and dogs barked in response. Sartes froze at the sound, but his father put a hand on his shoulder.

"We have to keep moving, Sartes."

They ran, but running hadn't been part of Sartes's plan. He tripped on one of the wires set out there, and pulled himself back to his feet only with difficulty. Somewhere behind them, he thought he could hear the sounds of the hunting party getting closer.

Sartes shook his head. "We can't outrun them. They have horses."

Already, he thought he could hear hooves. He *could* hear them, along with the whinnies of horses being pushed hard. He looked round for a stick, a stone, anything he could use as a weapon. He knew he couldn't really fight the army, but it was better to die fighting than in any of the ways he would die if they caught him.

Yet what he saw approaching was a single woman, riding one horse while leading two others. The horses looked like military mounts, complete with their riders' weapons and equipment, but the saddles were empty.

"Sartes?" she called out. "Berin?"

Sartes looked up in surprise, pressing closer to his father. "Who are you?"

"My name is Anka. There's no time to explain, but Ceres sent me. I'm with the rebellion. Quick, climb on before they realize that they're missing horses."

Sartes paused, looking back toward the camp.

"Do you want to risk them catching you?" Anka demanded.

She had a point. Even if they didn't know her, if she was claiming to be with the rebellion, then she was probably a friend. Picking one of the spare horses, Sartes climbed aboard. His father did the same with the other.

"I hope you two can ride," Anka said. "Because there's a *lot* of noise back there."

There was. On the edge of hearing, Sartes thought that he could hear more hooves, accompanied by shouts and horns. He saw Anka kick her mount into a run, and his father did the same.

Sartes took a breath. He was out. He'd found his father. He even had plans that would help the rebellion.

Now all he needed to do was survive.

CHAPTER TWENTY SEVEN

Thanos resisted the urge to punch the wall of the stables, but only just.

"Tell us the truth," he demanded of the stable boy who stood in front of him and Stephania.

He would have fought any number of opponents in the practice arena rather than spend another minute in frustrating investigation. He would have given anything he had to have an opponent in front of him, a problem that he could solve in a simple, honest way, rather than by skulking around, trying to unpick the intrigues of the court.

But he *didn't* have an opponent in front of him. That was the point. He was caught up in all this, and he wasn't sure how much time he had. Eventually, he was sure, someone would work out his new role with the rebellion, and that meant he only had a little while to find the person responsible for the attempt to kill him.

"I need an answer," Thanos said.

"It's all right," Stephania said, in a much more soothing tone that made Thanos glad he'd brought her for this. "We already know that Lucious gave you that amulet, didn't he? The one you used to prove to the Typhoon that you'd been sent by him?"

The stable hand looked away, but nodded.

"At least, I think so," he said. "He sent one of his servants. I was to take the amulet and deliver a message to the Typhoon."

"What message?" Thanos asked.

The stable boy shook his head. "I don't know. It was closed tight. I didn't want the Typhoon or Prince Lucious thinking that I was spying on them."

Even so, Thanos could guess what the message would have said. It was an order for his death, delivered without question by a foolish boy determined to impress.

"What... what happens now?" the stable boy asked.

Thanos could hear the fear there. The stable boy probably thought they were going to kill him for his part in the plot. Yet the truth was that he was no more than a tool used by someone else, and Thanos wasn't like Lucious. He found himself thinking of what Ceres would have done in a situation like this. It helped, even if it brought a pang of loss to him.

"You're going to stay quiet about us coming here," Thanos said. "Then, when the time comes, you're going to tell what you know to the court."

"I… I don't know…" the stable boy began.

Stephania gave him a hard look. "You will do everything that Thanos commands, won't you?"

The stable boy hung his head. "Yes."

"Good."

The two of them left together, and once they were outside the castle's stables, Thanos let himself relax a little. He turned to Stephania.

"Thank you for coming with me for that. I don't think he would have confirmed his story if you hadn't been there."

Stephania smiled. "I'm happy to help. I take it you want me to keep quiet about this for now?"

Thanos nodded. That was the other part of this investigation that he hated. For all that the king had promised his help, the truth was that they couldn't trust anyone at court. He didn't know who was involved in trying to kill him, and he had too many secrets about the rebellion to act out in the open. They had to keep up the façade of an investigation going nowhere, while at the same time conducting a real investigation in the background.

"No one will hear about it from me," Stephania promised. "Be careful?"

"I'll try," Thanos assured her. "Although I think the most dangerous thing happening in the castle in the next few days will be parties."

"Oh, parties can be more dangerous than you think," Stephania said. "Just don't do anything foolish like confronting Lucious, I mean."

"I won't," Thanos assured her. At least, not yet. They didn't have enough yet to accuse a prince of the Empire. They needed more proof, not least about why Lucious would do something like this in the first place.

It occurred to him that there was at least one avenue he hadn't explored yet. Cosmas the scholar had said that he had information for Thanos, but Thanos hadn't followed up on it yet. The old man had always been a good friend to him, and if he said that he had something for Thanos now, then Thanos believed it.

He walked to the castle library, making his way along the twisting corridors of the castle, trying to appear calm as he passed by servants and courtiers, acknowledging their nods and trying to make it look as though nothing was affecting him.

Thanos wasn't sure whether it was the need to find the assassin's employer that had made him suspicious, or his role with the rebellion now, but either way, he saw eyes everywhere in a way

123

he hadn't before. Every time he walked by a slave cleaning the marble of the castle floors, he found himself wondering who they reported to.

He hated the paranoia of his situation, but at the same time he needed it if he was going to stay alive here. There was so much at stake, and potentially so little time in which to do it all. He had to find out who was trying to kill him and why. He had to help the rebellion. More than all of that, he had to find a way to get Ceres back from the Isle of Prisoners. To do all of those things, he needed help.

When he made it to the library, Thanos paused. The library had always been a place Thanos enjoyed going. Its great doors were wide open, with shelves to either side, and desks set in quiet niches wherever they could fit. He found Cosmas in the library when he got there, standing in the middle of stacks of tomes, looking to Thanos like some mythical creature made of books from the waist down. Cosmas would probably consider that an improvement.

"Cosmas," Thanos said. "Are you looking for something?"

"Merely trying to undo some of the chaos that comes when the younger royals get into the library," the scholar replied. "Although it has meant I have been able to find scrolls that I haven't seen in twenty years."

Ordinarily, Thanos would have asked about them, and would probably have gotten a long lecture on some obscure subject as a result. Cosmas always seemed to learn about the oddest things. Once, Thanos had found him reading about the differences between two obscure types of beetle, neither of which was found in the Empire. When Thanos had asked why he wanted to know such a useless thing, he had answered simply that all knowledge was worth having.

Today, though, Thanos had no time for such distractions.

"You're here because of what I said to you," Cosmas said, emerging from behind his piles of books and scrolls.

"Yes, I want to know more about—"

"Wait," Cosmas said, and Thanos saw him go to the doors of the library, pushing them shut with a grunt of effort. He locked them too, using a large brass key that Thanos doubted had been used in a long time. Certainly, Thanos had never found the doors locked before.

"Now we can talk," Cosmas said. "The library is designed to be quiet. No one will overhear."

Thanos looked over to the scholar. "You said before that you knew something about who had tried to kill me and why?"

Cosmas nodded, gesturing for Thanos to follow as he headed into the shelves. "I can guess at the why," he said. "The who may come from that."

Thanos waited while the old man took out a book almost as large as he was, bound in calf-skin and edged in silver. Thanos helped him to carry it, but Cosmas was the one who fussed and cleared a space on one of the library's tables, then opened it to find the page he wanted.

Thanos looked down to find himself looking at a family tree. He recognized it instantly as the succession of the Empire. King Claudius was there, and Queen Athena. Lucious was there, with Thanos and his parents off to one side, where…

"Do you see it?" Cosmas asked.

Thanos saw it. There was an annotation in the margins.

"Ericthus, IV, 14-16? What does it mean?" he asked Cosmas. If there was anything written in the library the old man couldn't understand, Thanos hadn't found it yet.

"I believe Ericthus was a minor playwright in the reign of King Harrath," Cosmas explained.

"Two hundred years ago," Thanos said.

"Ah, so you did take in some of your studies after all."

Thanos doubted that a long dead playwright had anything to say about him, though. At least, not directly. But maybe someone was trying to say things indirectly, in a form that most people would just ignore.

"Do you have his plays here?" Thanos asked.

"Somewhere," Cosmas said, with a sweep of one wizened hand that took in the vast array of books scattered around. "I seem to remember them being next to a tome on the plant life of the outer islands."

Thanos suspected that wouldn't help much, but he set off hunting through the library anyway. Sometimes, even when a cause seemed lost, it was still worth trying. Like with Ceres. He would find a way to get her back. He had to.

For now, though, he dug through books and scrolls, trying to make sense of a system that probably only existed inside Cosmas's head. There was no method to it. He dug through works on the proper construction of aqueducts, philosophical scrolls, treatises on geometry… Finally, just as Cosmas had promised, he spotted a work on rare plants, and next to it, he saw a slender, leather-bound volume.

"I've got it!" Thanos said, holding the book aloft like it was the grand prize at the Stade after all that searching. He took it to the table, opening it to find an inscription inside.

Olivia, may you find as much happiness in Ericthus' work as I have. C.

Thanos froze at the sight of that name. His mother's name. And the initial, could that be... no, he couldn't think it.

Rather than stare at the inscription, he made himself turn to the fourth chapter, seeking out the first sixteen lines. They seemed to be a part of a speech by one of his characters, a noblewoman:

And should I hide the truth from all
That what should be done by my husband's hand
Has fallen instead to that of my king?

Thanos stared at the lines. Like the ones at the start of the book, they refused to sink in.

"This has to be some kind of joke," he managed at last.

"Not a joke," Cosmas said. "A reminder of another old story. Although this one isn't written down. King Claudius saw to that."

"What old story?" Thanos asked.

"That there was a midwife in the city who had heard things from the princess of the Empire she attended about her baby."

"You're talking about my mother," Thanos said. He'd never known enough about his mother or father to even imagine them. There were paintings in some of the galleries of the castle, but even those were stiff, formal things.

Cosmas nodded solemnly, his bald head dipping briefly so that Thanos could see the top of it.

"There have always been hints and stories," the scholar said. "But they faded, and you were just the king's nephew again."

"You're saying... you're saying that I'm the king's son." The enormity of that hit Thanos then. Everything he'd thought about the world seemed to unravel, all at once. All his life, despite everything, he'd known where he fit in, and who he was. Now, neither of those things seemed to be stable anymore.

He looked over at Cosmas, and a note of accusation crept into his voice. "If you know these stories, then you could have just told me."

"But then you would not have seen it for yourself. You do not just seek knowledge, Thanos. You seek proof."

Thanos still wasn't convinced. "You could have told me years ago."

"Some things are best left in the past. You were safer not knowing."

126

"But you don't think everyone has left them there," Thanos guessed.

Cosmas spread his hands. "I think someone found the book, and decided to remind themselves of their bloodline. They found a note in the margins, and they were more persistent than I could give them credit for. They learned about the old rumors. Perhaps they saw the beginnings of something they didn't want to happen."

"Who?" Thanos asked.

Cosmas smiled slightly. "You understand that I cannot say for certain. A wise man understands the limits of what he knows, and there have been many people in my library of late."

"Cosmas." That was sharper than Thanos intended. "I'm sorry, but my life's at stake."

"A lot more than your life, I think," Cosmas replied. "And to answer your question, Prince Lucious has been more diligent than usual with his studies."

Lucious again. Wherever he looked, it seemed as though Thanos was finding his name. The evidence was stacking up, but none of it seemed to be final.

"You said something about a midwife?" Thanos asked.

Cosmas nodded. "I didn't tell Lucious this part, but I was able to locate the woman. She lives in the city."

"I will need the address," Thanos said.

"Of course."

Thanos felt as though he was finally getting somewhere with his attempts to find out what was going on. He took the address from the scholar and practically ran from the library.

He forced himself to slow to a walk as he headed down to the stables, determined to ride down into the city and find the woman. He didn't want people to guess that something was wrong. He forced himself to make his way through the castle courtyard as calmly as if he were heading out for a pleasure ride, even though his every instinct said to run for the nearest horse and ride hard.

The stables were noisier than Thanos would have expected as he approached. Normally, there would have been the occasional whinny of the horses, a few good-natured shouts from the stable hands. Now, the horses sounded as though something had spooked them, clattering their hooves at the walls of their stalls, refusing to settle.

Thanos hurried to the stable doors, surprised to find them half open. No responsible stable hand would leave them like that. He looked inside, trying to make sense of it. The stables seemed to be empty of stable hands, the horses left to mill about in near panic.

In the middle of it all, Thanos saw the reason why.

"No," Thanos said, as he saw the body lying there. It was on its back, and Thanos instantly recognized the stable boy he'd interrogated earlier. The boy lay with his limbs spread wide, his eyes staring emptily upwards. There were bloody holes in the front of his tunic, but no slashes on his arms. He hadn't defended himself. Instead, someone he trusted had walked up to him and stabbed him.

No, not someone. Lucious was behind this. Thanos was sure of it. Anger rose in him, and a deep kind of sadness behind it. If he hadn't come to see this boy, would he still be alive? Had he brought this about? No, this was Lucious's fault. Everything pointed to Lucious.

Now, Thanos needed to find a way to prove it.

CHAPTER TWENTY EIGHT

Ceres stared up at the ziggurat of the forest folk. It was huge and ancient, obviously built long before their village, but still looking as though it belonged there. Beside her, Eoin stood waiting.

Steps led up the side, leading to the different levels of the structure. On each, one of the forest folk stood, or sat, or moved in elaborate dance fights with the air itself.

"What am I supposed to learn here?" Ceres said, and then caught herself. "I know, I know, everyone learns their own lessons. But how does this one work?"

"It's simple," Eoin said. "When you can meet me at the top, you will be ready."

"Ready for what?" Ceres demanded.

Eoin shrugged, with a smile that was far too infuriating. "I'll tell you that at the top."

He ran up the steps and Ceres made to follow, but the woman on the lowest tier of the ziggurat moved in front of her.

"First, you have things to learn. Do you know how to kick? Kick me."

Ceres thought she did, but the moment her foot struck out, the islander parried it away almost contemptuously. Her answering kick almost knocked Ceres from her feet. Ceres struck back, and again, she found it batted aside.

"This is all you can do?"

Ceres struck out again, and again. Each time, she missed, or found it blocked. Each time, a foot or a shin struck her. Before, she'd complained about not getting to fight. About having to move slowly and practice the movements over and over. Now, with her arms throbbing with bruises, Ceres was starting to wish for the dancelike slowness of the training before.

"Concentrate!" the forest woman in front of her snapped, making her point with a kick that whipped up to ruffle Ceres's hair.

Ceres guessed that she was supposed to copy and react, but when the forest folk were so much more skilled than her, it felt as though all she could do was get hit. A sideways kick slammed into her stomach, and Ceres gasped for air.

"How am I supposed to learn all this?" Ceres demanded. "You're not even showing me what you're doing."

"We show you every time we move," the woman countered. She spun, her foot flicking up again, and Ceres barely leaned back out of the way in time. "The world shows you with every breath."

Ceres did her best to copy, throwing kick after kick. She tried to mimic the form of it, but that didn't seem to be enough for her opponent.

"The outer skin of it doesn't matter," she snapped, kicking out at Ceres again. Ceres forced herself to push harder, hoping it would be enough.

Eventually, reluctantly, the woman let her pass. By the time she did, Ceres felt as though she could barely stand, and the act of pulling herself up to the next step took all she had. She wasn't even sure how much she'd learned from the endless, exhausting repetition.

And that was just the first step.

There was a man on the next who jabbed at the body's vulnerable points with bark-covered fingers. Ceres threw one of the kicks she'd learned at him, and he struck down painfully on her knee.

"That is not what you are here to learn."

So she had to start again, with the only way to learn her own pain. She copied as best she could, but it still seemed like forever before she could haul herself to the next tier, then the next. There was a woman who threw her effortlessly to the ground, a man who struck with his elbows and knees, impossible to retreat from.

She didn't see the point of it. She couldn't learn all this in one attempt, no matter how much she'd been training with Eoin. All she was doing was getting so bruised that she could barely make it from one tier to the next.

She stood, ready for her next opponent, her next teacher, and found herself facing a girl barely older than Eike, so deeply enmeshed in the islanders' curse that her skin seemed more bark than flesh.

"I'm supposed to fight you?" Ceres asked.

The girl laughed. "It's not about fighting, silly. No wonder you're getting hit so much. It's about understanding. You know, I bet I could push you right off this ziggurat if I tried."

She tried, and Ceres had to dodge out of the way of the push. Then the girl caught her arm, twisting, and Ceres had to roll to take the pressure off.

"Can you feel the forest?" the girl asked, in between pushes. "Eoin says you will, but I don't know. You're getting hit a *lot*."

She kept attacking, in a strange mixture of pushes, trips, and twisting joint locks that meant Ceres could never quite get her balance, never quite attack.

"You've got to learn the lessons the world has," the girl said, with another laugh. "You've got to be part of it. Relax."

Ceres did her best, even though it seemed strange to take lessons from someone so much younger than her. She managed to twist out of the way of the next push, but the one after that caught her, sending her to the edge of the step she was on. For a moment, she teetered on the edge, looking out over the village and the jungle below. It was a surprise to see just how high she'd climbed by then, with the rest of it spread out like some green carpet.

She felt the breath of the wind there, seeming to hold her against the side of the ziggurat as it came in off the jungle. It felt as though the whole thing was breathing like one giant organism, pulsing with life.

"Don't think, move," the girl said, and aimed a push at Ceres that would have sent her off the edge to tumble to the forest below if she hadn't stepped aside.

She was so tired by now that she did it without thinking, energy rising within her automatically. It felt then as though she could feel everything around her. She could see the flow of the next push, timed in rhythm with the endless pulse of the jungle. Ceres fit into the flow of that push, moved neatly into the space it created, and timed a push of her own that sent the girl spinning and laughing.

"Good. You can go up."

The next step had a massive man whose legs were halfway to being tree trunks, and who threw punches Ceres suspected would have killed her if she hadn't been flooded by the power that lay within her. She struck back, and although her opponent didn't move, he seemed satisfied.

The one after that was a woman who grabbed Ceres, dragging her to the ground. Ceres felt the opening and rolled, coming up behind her, throwing an arm around her opponent's throat and squeezing.

On and on it went. Each of the forest folk seemed to have a different skill, but Ceres was starting to see that they weren't so different after all. Whether they punched or kicked, danced around her or charged forward to grapple with her, all of the islanders moved in tune with the world around them, no thought or form to it beyond that of the moment. With energy flooding through her, Ceres found it easy to relax into the same moment, and one by one they let her rise up the slopes of the ziggurat.

Finally, Ceres climbed to the top of the structure, where Eoin was waiting. Up here, Ceres could see a ribbon of water that poured down the rear slope of the ziggurat, coming from a spring that arched over a block of stone, tumbling down in a waterfall easily as powerful as the one they'd trained beneath before. Ceres couldn't see beyond that curtain of water, but she was certain there was something.

Eoin stood before the wall of water. He stood there looking as perfect as a statue.

He gave her a questioning look. "Do you understand yet? Can you feel it, Ceres?"

Ceres nodded. She could feel the whole world around her as she stood up there. She could see the island spread out below them too, looking even more beautiful from here than it did at ground level. She could see the streams and lagoons there, the inlets and the beaches that edged onto the jungle. This high, she could feel the wind whipping around her too, swirling as they stood there together.

"The first time I saw you, I knew you had power," Eoin said. "I thought that our ways might lead you to it." He smiled. "And now I see that I was right."

Ceres stood there, and she could feel the energy pulsing from within her.

"There are some things that cannot be controlled," Eoin continued. "You might as well try to control the jungle. But you do have a choice. You can choose to develop the power within you. Or you can choose to let it disappear."

Ceres frowned at him then. "Why would I do that?"

Eoin sighed.

"Because the power within you is a dangerous one," he said. "It is a very old gift, and if you choose to accept it, it will grow within you. You will hurt or kill all those who attempt to harm you. Anyone who touches you with malice will turn to stone."

Ceres thought back to the moments in the Stade when her power had come to her, killing creatures that had been on the verge of tearing her to pieces. She thought of the creature that had attacked their ship, and the way it had recoiled from her.

"That doesn't sound like a bad thing," she said.

"Perhaps not," Eoin replied. "But it is like keeping a wild animal to protect yourself. It might be fiercely loyal, but you will not be able to hold it back from others. It will strike at anyone who touches you in anger, whether you want them to be hurt or not. It could hurt those you love. And once your power has been revealed, it cannot be contained."

That was a harder thing, and it was enough to make Ceres pause.

132

"Do I have to do this?" she asked.

Eoin shook his head. "You've already learned a lot about fighting from us. Perhaps that's what you were brought here to do. Perhaps it's *all* you were brought here to do."

"But you don't believe that," Ceres guessed.

Eoin held out his hand to her. Ceres took it, feeling the mossy smoothness of his skin where they touched.

"I think that there are many places you could have learned to fight, but very few where you can go deeper. Where you can learn to understand what lies within you. I think you were brought here for a reason."

She stood there, her heart pounding, fearing to embrace her power—yet craving it.

Eoin stepped back.

"The decision is yours."

Ceres stood, looking out over the village. She looked further out, to where the ocean lapped at the edges of the island. Somewhere beyond it, her family was waiting. She wanted to get back to them. She wanted to have the strength to protect them. The rebellion was out there too. They needed her to have the strength to make a difference.

But did it need her to unleash something like this? How many people might she hurt? How many people might she kill? This was a decision that couldn't be undone. The kind of decision that might affect her whole life.

She saw Eoin step through the wall of water at the top of the ziggurat, disappearing beyond it. His voice carried back.

"Follow me if you dare, Ceres."

Ceres stood there for a long time. She thought of the rebellion, and of all the people who had been taken away by the Empire. She thought of her family. Then she thought of Thanos, dead because of all this madness. Madness that she might finally have the power to stop if she accepted this.

Ceres felt the water thunder down on her as she stepped through it.

133

CHAPTER TWENTY NINE

Thanos walked down into the poorest districts of Delos, trying not to let the pity he felt at the state of this quarter of the city show on his face. He kept his cloak wrapped around him so that no one would see who he was. He doubted that being a prince would carry much weight here amongst those so poor they couldn't even afford food.

The houses down here barely even merited the term. They weren't so much discrete units as agglomerations of wood and plaster, one shack flowing into the next until Thanos couldn't tell where the buildings started and stopped.

There were beggars on the street, and Thanos guessed that there would have been thieves too if anyone had possessed anything worth stealing. He kept a wary eye on the alleys he passed while he tried to find the one that matched the address he had for the midwife.

He looked behind him too. It wasn't just thieves he had to worry about. After what had happened to the stable boy, he didn't want to risk bringing death down on anyone else.

Even with the address Cosmas had given him, it took time to find the right place. The address was for a house in one of the city's poorest neighborhoods. Thanos slipped down there in the early morning light, wrapping himself in his cloak so he wouldn't attract attention.

He found the house after more than an hour of searching. It was ramshackle and dilapidated, looking to Thanos as though the spider webs were the only things keeping one of the walls standing. There was a faint smell of rot there as he got closer, and it was so quiet that Thanos wasn't sure whether it was empty or not.

He knocked anyway, and was a little surprised when a woman his own age answered the door.

"I'm looking for the woman who was a midwife up at the castle two decades ago," he said. The young woman looked as though she might bolt, but when Thanos threw the hood of his cloak back, she seemed to freeze in place. She obviously recognized him.

"Please," he said. "It's important."

She stood there considering him for a moment. "You're…"

"Yes," Thanos said with a nod. "I am."

"You want my mother. Come with me."

Thanos followed her into a shack that didn't look much better on the inside than the outside. The little furniture that there was looked as though it had been there a long time. It certainly didn't look like the home of a midwife successful enough to be summoned to the palace.

In a back room, he found an old woman sitting on a chair that looked as though it might fall apart at any moment. As soon as he saw her hands, crabbed with arthritis, Thanos understood why the two weren't living anywhere better.

"Be gentle with Mother," the young woman said. "Her memory isn't what it was. She hardly speaks now."

Thanos made his way over. There was no response from the old woman. He crouched down beside her, but her expression didn't change.

"I need your help," Thanos said. "I found a reference in the castle library, in a genealogy. I'm trying to find out why."

There was no response from the woman.

"It was to a collection of plays," Thanos tried. Still, there was no response.

"Please," Thanos said. "People have been trying to kill me, and I think this has something to do with it. I need to understand the reason why."

There wasn't any answer from the old woman. There barely seemed to be any spark of life there, so that it seemed to Thanos as though he might be talking to an empty shell.

The seconds stretched out, turning into minutes. He looked into the woman's eyes, silently pleading for something.

"Please," he said. "I just want to understand who I really am."

This was hopeless. He would never find out what he needed to know.

He stood with a sigh. "I'm sorry to have bothered you. I'll go."

He turned, and found a hand clamped onto his arm. The old woman's fingers felt fragile around his wrist, but Thanos could feel the strength there too.

Thanos saw her eyes lock onto his as he turned back. "The son of the king."

Thanos shook his head. "I'm sorry, but I'm the king's—"

"Son," the old woman said, cutting him off in a voice that sounded rusty with lack of use. "The girl pretended that you weren't at first, but he was right there outside the room, pacing the way only a father can."

"You're sure?" Thanos asked.

The former midwife nodded. "She told me, because there wasn't anyone else to tell."

Thanos swallowed as he tried to make sense of it. Even though he'd guessed at this with Cosmas, it was still a shock to hear it like this, from a woman who'd been there. There was a part of him that still wanted to say that it was a lie, but it made more sense than he'd thought it would. The shock still hit him like a falling boulder, but there was something about it that seemed right too.

He stood there while the pieces fell into place. If this old woman was telling the truth, then he really was the heir. And that gave Lucious more than enough reasons to want him dead.

Anger rose in Thanos then, hard edged as diamond. He'd put up with so much of what Lucious had done over the years. He'd stood by while he'd been the worst kind of noble, while he'd put Thanos down, even while he'd attacked Ceres. Well, no more.

"Thank you," Thanos said to the old woman. "I have to get back to the castle."

"Don't thank me, boy," he heard her say. "There's some news that brings no one happiness."

***

Thanos stormed his way back to the castle, ignoring the guards who tried to challenge him at the gates. He made his way along the corridors, heading back to his rooms only because it would give him a chance to fetch his weapons and armor. Right then, he could have walked up to Lucious and ripped him in half with his bare hands, after all he'd done.

He threw open the doors to his rooms, and was surprised to see Stephania sitting in there on a couch, obviously waiting for him. She stood with a frown as soon as he came in.

"Thanos? What's wrong?"

"How did you get in here?" Thanos asked. Too much of his anger came through in that.

"A servant let me in," Stephania said. "There were things I needed to tell you, and I thought it was better to wait for you in here. But that can wait. What's happened?"

Thanos stood there, with his hands balled up. "I found out the truth."

"What truth?" Stephania asked.

Thanos paused for a moment before he told her, but he had to say this to someone. "Lucious is the one who tried to kill me."

"Oh, Thanos," Stephania said, and Thanos saw her raise her hand to her mouth. He knew how she felt.

"I'm going to kill him," Thanos said. "After everything he's done, I'm going to kill him, Stephania."

She stepped between him and the door.

"Don't try to stop me," Thanos said.

"It's not that," Stephania replied. "It's… I have some news."

"It can wait."

He saw her shake her head. "It *can't* wait. It's about Ceres."

That was enough to stop Thanos in his tracks. He stood there in silence.

"You should come and sit down," Stephania said, moving back to the couch and gesturing for him to join her.

Thanos didn't want to. He wanted the news now, whatever it was, but it seemed clear that Stephania wasn't going to say anything until he joined her. He sat down carefully, feeling the hardness of the couch beneath him.

"Don't tell me…" Thanos began.

"They were taking her to the Isle of Prisoners on a prison ship. That ship never arrived."

Thanos thought of all the possibilities. Maybe the rebellion had intercepted the ship. Maybe Akila's people had captured it. Maybe Ceres had orchestrated an escape.

"When a boat passed close to their path, they found wreckage," Stephania said. "They say there must have been a storm. The ship was torn apart. There were… I'm sorry, Thanos, but there were no survivors."

"No," Thanos said, shaking his head. He stood up. "No, it can't be."

Ceres couldn't be dead. She *couldn't* be. If she was dead, then nothing else made sense. Thanos felt tears welling up in his eyes, impossible to stop no matter how hard he tried. He made to turn away so that Stephania wouldn't see, but she was there in front of him anyway.

She wrapped her arms around him, holding him close enough that he could smell the soft, floral scent of her.

"I'm sorry," she said. "I wanted to be the one to tell you. I didn't trust anyone else to do it."

"It's…" He didn't know what to say next. He just didn't know. It felt as though the world had come to a jarring halt, caught between one moment and the next. It felt as though he'd breathed out, and fresh air refused to come into his lungs, leaving him as some kind of gasping wreck.

Stephania was there in that space, holding onto him, feeling like an anchor to the world when so much of Thanos felt as though he was floating free. Her hand felt so small and delicate in his, but there was strength there as she held onto him. She was there while his grief washed over him, building in waves that he wouldn't have wanted anyone else to see.

Stephania held onto him through all of it, and Thanos found himself more and more grateful for the fact that she was there. She was right; there was no one else there who could have told him something such as this. There was no one else he would have trusted to hold him like this.

And he *did* trust her. Stephania had been there to help him through his investigation. She'd put aside the way he'd treated her, and she was there now in the darkest moment of his life. She didn't say anything. She didn't need to. She was simply there, waiting while Thanos's grief burned itself out. He was surprised to find what was there as the initial rush of it passed.

He'd never thought he could feel anything for someone like Stephania, but now, looking at her, it was impossible not to. She was perfect in so many ways, but this moment just went to show exactly how deeply he understood her.

Thanos realized how close they were then. Close enough that it would have been nothing to close the distance between them. It would have been so easy to kiss her then, and maybe that would have helped. Maybe, he thought, it would be enough to make him feel something, anything, instead of the awful emptiness that yawned inside him.

Instead, he felt her fingers touch his lips.

"Don't," Stephania said. "Not like this. You're upset. I don't want it to be just because of that, and it's not why I'm doing this. I'm here because you're my friend, and because I care about you."

The amazing thing was just how much he cared about her too. It felt like it had crept up on Thanos, feelings for Stephania building up within him almost imperceptibly the more time he spent with her. He'd gotten to see who she really was, and it was someone he could easily find himself falling in love with.

Someone he could find himself being with forever.

"You need to concentrate on the important things," Stephania said. "Like what you're going to do next."

"That part's simple," Thanos said. "I'm going to deal with Lucious."

CHAPTER THIRTY

Sartes clung to the horse tightly as they raced toward the city, terrified that he might fall off if he didn't. Just as terrified that he might drop the precious plans he held. He reined in his horse, and beside him, Anka and his father did the same.

"Anka, we have to go slower," he said. "I can't risk dropping these."

"What's more important than your life?" Anka called back.

"Sartes has plans taken from the Empire's command tents," his father said, answering for him.

Sartes saw Anka stare over at him in obvious surprise.

"Really? You have their plans?"

Sartes nodded. "One of the commanders wanted them so he could see where he was supposed to go. I took everything I could."

"Then we can't just take you into the city the normal way," Anka said. "Follow me."

She heeled her horse into a gallop and Sartes did his best to follow. He dared a glance back, and now he could see horses on the horizon, dust flying from their hooves. They'd spent too much time talking. The soldiers were in sight.

Sartes did his best to stay on the horse as Anka led the way down back trails and over broken ground. He looked over to see his father urging his horse on, and tried not to show how scared he was then. If the soldiers could see them, it had turned from a hunt into a race, and he didn't know if he could win it.

Sartes followed Anka along a twisting series of trails that led through a stand of trees and past a spot where two boulders stood at either side, almost blocking the path. It seemed to Sartes that it was a route designed to confuse and distract those following, but it meant that he was jolted with every rut and shift of ground.

"Not far now," he heard Anka call. "We'll have to let the horses go when we get to the city, but our people have a way in."

Our people. Sartes liked the sound of that. He'd wanted to be a part of the rebellion since the first time he'd heard about it. He'd wanted to be there for the attack on Fountain Square. If he'd been older...

...then maybe he would have ended up dead, like Rexus and his brother. He'd been too young to do anything for the rebellion before, but maybe he could now.

He saw a creek ahead, steep sided and too fast flowing to risk plunging into, especially with the plans. Anka's horse jumped it easily, and Sartes saw his father follow. His horse seemed to know what was required of it without being told, giving Sartes no time to think about just how wide the gap was, or how cold the water would be if he fell.

He felt the muscles of the horse bunch beneath him and he gripped it with his thighs as it leapt. For a moment, everything felt weightless, then the ground came thundering up to meet them, and Sartes was almost jarred from the saddle. He felt the plans he held shifting, grabbed for them, and managed to keep them from falling as his horse surged forward again.

In the distance, Sartes saw the walls of Delos. Given the misery of the city, he had never thought he would be so grateful to see them again. The three of them rode toward the walls, and Anka angled a mirror toward the sun in a pattern that seemed to repeat as they got closer.

They rode in through a side gate and Sartes dared another glance back. The soldiers chasing them were closer now, swords out ready to fight, their horses straining as they charged after the three of them.

They raced through the streets, to a crossroads thronging with people. To Sartes's surprise, one waved.

"Dismount here!" Anka said, practically leaping off her horse.

Sartes and his father followed her lead, and almost before he was off the horse, Sartes found the reins being taken by a man in simple clothes, the hilts of weapons just visible as they moved. Another man threw a worn and filthy cloak his way.

"Put it on!" Anka ordered, donning one that was almost identical.

Wearing them, Sartes, his father, and Anka looked to Sartes like a group of beggars making their way through the city. The crowd closed around them and he saw the soldiers riding through, shoving people out of the way. Briefly, Sartes's heart was in his mouth. What if their disguise didn't work? What if the men spotted the three of them?

But they rode past, while Sartes and the others made their way along the city's streets. Anka led the way, taking twists and turns that seemed to make no sense until they reached a space with a walled courtyard. Anka headed inside, then up into a building that mixed stone and timber, more solid than most of those around it.

Sartes followed. His father put a hand on his shoulder.

"We did it. We actually got away."

Sartes nodded, and relief flooded through him. "You saved me."

His father shook his head. "Anka saved both of us."

"And now maybe we can repay her," Sartes said, fingering the maps he still held.

He followed while Anka led the way up to an attic-level room where more than a dozen people were waiting for them. They stood around a large table, the space lit by guttering candles.

The surprising thing to Sartes was how ordinary they all looked. He'd heard so many stories of the rebellion that he was expecting something... more. Perhaps an army of combatlords, each ready to take on a horde of the Empire's soldiers. Skilled assassins, cloaked in black and armed with rare poisons. Heroic leaders like Rexus.

Instead, they just seemed to be normal people. People like his father. People like him. They didn't seem happy.

"Anka, what were you thinking riding in here in such a hurry?" one man asked. He had the broad shoulders of a farmer, and a rough beard. "You could have compromised everything here."

"Were you followed?" a shorter man asked. He fingered the hilt of a knife. "Will we need to fight?"

"We weren't followed," Anka assured him. "And there was no time for anything else. We have something to show you."

Sartes let her take the plans from him, then helped her to spread them out on the table.

"As you know, I've been looking for Ceres's brother Sartes," Anka said.

"Wasting time," a woman said, "when everyone's sons and brothers are at risk."

It was hard for Sartes to like someone who thought finding him was a waste of time.

"Not wasting time, Hannah," Anka shot back. "I found him. And he brought us these. Plans showing the Empire's intentions. They show which of our bases they know about, and which they intend to move against. We even have the orders to tell us when they plan to get there."

"So we have plenty of time to evacuate our people," the first rebel to speak said.

"That's one possibility," Anka said.

"What's the alternative?"

Sartes understood, even if the others didn't. "We could ambush them."

"You're Sartes?" Hannah asked.

Sartes nodded.

"So we owe you a great deal for getting these papers, but that doesn't mean you know about tactics or strategy."

Sartes shrugged. "Only as much as I learned in the army."

"As a conscript," the woman countered. "I doubt they teach you much about planning."

"They teach you how to stay alive," Sartes said. "You learn about your enemies. You guess what they're going to do before they do it, so that they can't hurt you."

He paused as he realized that everyone's eyes were on him. He almost couldn't keep going, but then he felt his father's hand on his shoulder. That presence was enough to give him the confidence to keep going.

"I know what the army is like better than any of you," Sartes said. "I can tell you which of the officers will rush in, and which will be cautious. I can tell you that the conscripts will run, if you give them any real prospect of escaping. We can ambush them. We can win."

"It's what we need to do," Anka said, adding her voice to his. "We can't fight them head on, so what's left? We either sit back and wait to be destroyed, or we take chances like this one."

"Do we have enough people?" one of the rebels asked.

"We have some," Anka said.

"You'll have more if you free the conscripts," Sartes said. "They hate the Empire. The ones who don't fight for you will run."

"And we fight smart," Anka insisted. "Look here. If they want to get to our people to the north of the city, that means going through the burial grounds here and here. We know there are catacombs to strike from where they can't see us. And if we do it here, we have the ruins of the old mausoleums to use. We could bring walls down right on them. Then we have tripwires, pits… we could halve their numbers before it even came to fighting."

"They're still better armed and armored than us," Hannah insisted.

Sartes pointed to his father. "My father is the best smith you will ever meet. He can help you to make all the weapons you will ever need."

Sartes saw his father nod. "That's true. Give me metal, a fire, and enough people to help, and I can produce whatever you need."

"How quickly?" Anka asked.

His father seemed to consider for a moment. "That will depend on what kind of resources you can give me. But if you give me enough people, I can equip you as well as the army. Better."

"And we don't need enough to take them all on at once," Anka pointed out. "We just need enough people and weaponry to hit the weakest forces. We can hit supply centers to take more. Look. We could evacuate the people in the old quarter, leave traps behind, and hit their supply train while they're still looking for us."

She started to outline her plans, and Sartes had to admit he was impressed. He'd expected things to be difficult for the rebellion without Rexus there, but Anka seemed to understand every detail. In some ways, Sartes thought, she was an even better choice than Rexus. Where the rebels' former leader might have charged in, Anka seemed more cautious, wanting to plan everything as carefully as possible to ensure that their people weren't hurt.

Somewhere in all the planning, Sartes drifted to the back of the room. His father was there, and he put an arm around his son's shoulders. For the first time since the soldiers had taken him as a conscript, he actually felt safe.

"It sounds as though there's going to be a lot of work to come," his father said.

Sartes nodded. "I don't mind that. I *want* to help the rebellion."

"Are you sure?" his father asked. "It's already cost me one son. You could go and be safe."

"Would you go?" Sartes asked.

His father shook his head. "They need me to make weapons for them. But you could get away."

"Where?" Sartes asked. "Where is there that's safe? Anywhere I go, the army could come and take me, or kill me just because they feel like it. The only way to be safe is if we help everyone, and I *want* to help everyone. There are still plenty of others like me stuck in the army, or getting attacked every day out there."

His father nodded. "I'm proud of you, son, and you're right. We have to make this better. I guess I can do that making weapons."

"And I'll do whatever I can to help," Sartes said.

He wasn't sure what he would do yet, but he was sure of one thing: this time, when the time came to fight the Empire, he wanted to be there.

CHAPTER THIRTY ONE

The wall of water gushed over Ceres, so cold that it made her shiver. As it poured across her, it felt as though it was washing away some block or barrier, letting something open up inside her like a flower.

She'd passed the islanders' test. She'd learned the lessons they wanted her to learn. Even now, she could hear the whisper of the island in the background, pulsing like one living thing. For a moment, her own power pulsed in response, and the strength of it was enough that Ceres couldn't concentrate.

Only Eoin's voice brought her back to herself, letting Ceres see that she was in a stone-walled tunnel, which sloped down sharply in a long spiral. She couldn't tell if it was natural or if it had been carved out by the hands of the islanders.

"This way," Eoin said, and Ceres could see him a little way ahead.

She followed him down it by the faint sunlight that seemed to reflect from the walls. The tunnel twisted and turned, so that soon, Ceres wasn't sure if they were still under the ziggurat, or somewhere else entirely.

Ahead, Ceres thought she could see a square of sunlight, with Eoin briefly silhouetted against it as he stepped out into it. Ceres followed, stepping through another curtain of water, this one a trickle compared to the previous one.

She stepped out onto grass, into a giant, bowl-shaped depression. Trees hung over the rim at improbable angles, clinging to the rock as they stuck out. Ceres found herself wondering how many were forest folk who had succumbed to the curse.

There were forest folk there, building a bonfire at one side of the open space with driftwood and deadfall. There were others setting out food and drink, obviously preparing a feast from forest fruits and fish from the shores.

"We shall celebrate your accepting your power," Eoin said.

"And afterwards?" Ceres asked.

Eoin held out a hand for Ceres to take. "That is up to you. You can stay with us for as long as you wish. You can return to the Empire to fight. Or you can go another way if you choose. We will help you, wherever you want to go."

At the very center of the bowl-shaped depression, there was a ring of what looked like wooden posts, surrounding a plinth. Yet, as she got closer, Ceres could see the eyes in the posts, moving even though the rest of them couldn't.

"In the last stages before the curse claims them fully, our people are connected to the jungle more than ever," Eoin said. "They see things that the rest of us don't. We come here for the most important decisions."

Ceres walked with him into that circle, feeling the eyes upon her. The forest folk gathered around now, their bonfire burning in the background.

There was a bowl on the plinth. Eoin lifted it, offering it to her. It was sweet smelling and sticky looking. He pressed it into her hands.

"If you want to accept the power within you, drink. Drink and see."

"Drink and see what?" Ceres asked.

Eoin spread his hands. "Everything."

She took the bowl and sipped at it, then drank it down swiftly. No one there was going to try to hurt her. At least, not in ways that didn't involve the normal rough and tumble of fighting. The drink was sticky and thick, tasting of sweet berries and the sap of jungle plants as she drank it.

"What's in this?" Ceres asked, but Eoin just smiled. Ceres looked around, and the flames of the bonfire seemed to swim.

She heard a repetitive thudding, and for a moment she thought that maybe a drummer had started to play. Then she realized that it was the rhythmic pounding of the forest folk's feet, stamping in perfect time. It seemed to join with the ever louder beating of her heart.

It seemed impossibly slow, but then, so did the rest of the world. It seemed to Ceres as if the dancers were drifting along like leaves in the firelight, every movement so slow and precise that it felt as though they were barely dancing at all.

The world seemed to swim, and Ceres felt herself falling. Eoin was there beside her, laying her down gently on the jungle floor.

"Sleep, Ceres," he said. "Sleep, and dream."

Ceres stared up at him for a breath or two longer. It was a good last sight before she closed her eyes.

Delos spread out below her like some child's toy. It seemed as though she was drifting toward the city, down and down, ever closer. Ceres could feel the rush of the air through her fingers, but she didn't feel as though she was falling. She certainly didn't feel in any danger.

She fell closer, and she realized that she was falling toward her former home. Almost as soon as she realized that, the scene shifted, and she found herself looking at two people it took her a second to recognize.

Her mother and father looked so much younger there; younger than Ceres had ever seen them. She could see a tiny boy toddling about, and knew it had to be her older brother, Nesos. The two of them were looking down into a crib.

"What have you done?" her mother asked.

"What I had to do," her father replied.

"If you think that we're going to take in some brat, then—"

"That's exactly what we're going to do," her father insisted. "We will raise her as our own, and never give her any reason to think otherwise."

Ceres wanted to look closer, but the images in front of her shifted again.

Now, there were armies clashing around her, the clash of blades mixing in with the screams of the dying and the thud of armored bodies slamming into one another. She saw people struggling against each other, stabbing and slashing as they fought for room.

She saw herself at the heart of it, dressed in gold-edged armor, wielding a sword and shield. A man ran at her and she stepped aside, slicing with her sword. She heard herself shouting orders over the chaos of the melee, and to her surprise, those around her listened. They reformed, charged, and fought again.

Ceres saw herself at the heart of the fight, her opponents falling until finally they turned and ran, the rout spreading out from the point where she fought until it encompassed all of the opposing forces. Ceres heard the battle cry of her soldiers repeated over and over.

"Ceres! Ceres!"

Ceres stood there, not understanding. What was happening? Were these just random images, or was there more to them?

"You know what they are, Ceres."

Ceres turned, and she wasn't standing in a battlefield anymore. She might have been back on the island again, but this island was different. Where the forest folk's home was covered in the green of the jungle, here rainbow marble stood up in spires and arches above flat meadows.

A woman stood there, or at least the vague impression of a woman. She wore what looked to Ceres like a cloak at first glance, but it was more than that. It was like a haziness she couldn't quite see through; a gap in the vision that she couldn't pierce.

"Who are you?" Ceres demanded. "What are you?"

"A vision, an image," the woman said.

"An image of what?" Ceres wasn't going to let it go.

The woman tilted her head to one side, the cowl over it shifting in response.

"Of your mother."

The woman reached out toward her, and Ceres stood still as she touched Ceres's brow. The power within her flared with that touch, and Ceres felt it like a living thing inside her. In that moment, it seemed to burst up through her, pouring out of her like dark smoke until it hung above her in a cloud.

The female figure seemed to regard it. She reached out, shaping the smoke between her hands like clay, twisting it into strands and reshaping it into something else. It seemed to grow as she did it, becoming something different, something more.

"Do you choose this?" the female figure asked.

Ceres nodded. "Yes."

"Then be what you should be."

It poured back into Ceres then, and now it seemed to fill her to bursting point. It was there in her, and it was her, all at once. The power of it seemed to overwhelm her in that moment, and Ceres fell. The hidden woman caught her, laying her down gently.

"When you wake, come and find me," she said.

"Where?" Ceres asked.

"The Isle Beyond the Mist."

Ceres wanted to ask what she meant, and where it, was, but in that moment she felt the vision starting to fade. She dropped back into wakefulness, and realized she was lying on the grass by the bonfire.

She saw Eoin looking down at her, in obvious concern.

The aches and pains of her fights had faded, the power within her just below the surface. She let Eoin help her up.

She still stood within a circle of the forest folk, and she could see the way they watched her now. She knew that they could see the new power within her, the same way that she could feel them all joined in their connection with the island.

Slowly, they started to chant, and it took Ceres a moment to realize what it was that they were chanting, slow and solemn, as if a great leader were amongst them.

"Ceres, Ceres, Ceres!"

CHAPTER THIRTY TWO

Thanos had made his way to the king's chambers many times in his life, but he doubted he'd ever felt as much as he did now. Anger, betrayal, but also a strange sense of having found some kind of completion. All of them vied for space within him as he strode toward the entrance.

The doors there were extravagant things, like so much of the rest of the castle, covered in painted carvings depicting scenes of battle and judgment. When he was younger, Thanos had traced them with his hands, imagining all the great deeds of kings long dead. Now, he saw them for what they were: a boast, a message.

A guard stood at either side of the doors, in armor that practically dripped in gold, given their status as royal bodyguards. One raised a hand as Thanos approached.

"I'm sorry, your highness, but the king is not receiving visitors."

Thanos fixed him with a look. Normally, he would have argued or tried to persuade. He understood that this man was just trying to do his job, but right then, nothing was going to keep him from speaking with King Claudius.

With his father. Just the thought of that was enough to send a fresh wave of emotion running through him.

"Step aside," Thanos said, and the guards must have heard something in his voice, because they hurriedly moved out of the way. That was good. In spite of everything, Thanos didn't want to hurt *them*.

He pushed open the doors. Inside, he found King Claudius drinking, attended by serving girls while he chewed on a chicken leg. He sat on an elegantly carved chair in front of a roaring fire, with a gaming board in front of him, the counters there suggesting a game already in progress.

Thanos saw the king look up as he entered. He saw the initial flash of anger soften at the sight of him, and now Thanos could guess why.

"Thanos, I thought I said I wasn't to be disturbed. But no matter. Join me. Normally, the only way I can get a good game is to play myself."

Thanos stood there, looking around at the servants. "Everybody get out." When they didn't move, he raised his voice. "Leave, I said."

He watched the servants run for the door, then waited for the thud of it swinging shut. King Claudius stood, and for the first time in a while Thanos looked, really looked, at him. He found himself searching the king's face, picking out features and looking for similarities. Was the arch of that brow the same as his? The slight raise of the cheekbones?

Right now, it seemed as though the main thing that they had in common was their anger. King Claudius was reddening with it, and Thanos saw his arm sweep out to knock away the gaming pieces.

"How dare you dismiss my servants? Have you forgotten who is the king here, Thanos?"

"I have not forgotten," Thanos said. On another day, he might have bowed or knelt, but not today.

"And storming in here. Who do you think you are to do such a thing?"

"I think I am your son," Thanos said, and each word felt like a stone slab being put down. He hadn't been sure how he would say it, but now that he had, it couldn't be taken back.

The energy of the anger seemed to drain from the room as quickly as it had come. If Thanos hadn't already had confirmation of who he was, that would have done it, with no need for the king to say anything. Even so, he wanted to hear King Claudius admit it.

The king staggered back into his chair, falling there as heavily as if Thanos had shoved him. He reached for his wine cup, then threw it into the fire. Thanos heard it clatter against the coals, the wine hissing as it steamed.

"What have you heard?" King Claudius demanded. "*Where* have you heard it?"

Thanos thought of the midwife, then of the dead stable hand. He wasn't going to bring trouble to anyone else. Even Cosmas might be in danger if Thanos explained too much about how he'd learned the truth.

"Does that matter?" Thanos countered. "What matters is that I'm your son. Aren't I?"

King Claudius looked down at the remains of his game for what seemed like a long time before he finally answered.

"Yes. Your mother... she was so beautiful. When I learned that she was pregnant, I was so happy, but I couldn't admit it. Neither of us could. It would have torn things apart. Instead, we hid things."

Thanos thought of the references left in the book of genealogy. The king might have ordered it hidden, but his mother had clearly intended that it should come out at some point. That, or she simply wanted the comfort of being able to put the truth down somewhere.

149

"So, I am your son," Thanos said. "Your eldest son."

"And my finest," King Claudius said. "You are all that I could have hoped you might be. You are clever, skilled in war, diligent, able to command those around you. You were victorious in the Stade when Lucious ran, and I couldn't have been prouder of you then. When I thought you were lost in the war, something broke inside me. When you came back, it was like the sun returning after a long winter."

Thanos wasn't sure what to say to that. He hadn't heard the king speak that warmly of him in a long time, and King Claudius had been the one to send him to war in the first place. It meant a lot to be the king's son, but he still wasn't sure *what* it meant, because this man was still cruel, still a tyrant to his people.

"I'm glad that I finally know the truth," Thanos said. "I feel like I know who I am for the first time."

"You have always been my son," the king said. "Even though you didn't know it, you have always been a man I could have wished to be."

Thanos was more than that though, wasn't he? "If I'm your son, am I your heir?"

King Claudius nodded. "And that is one reason we couldn't speak of it. It would have torn the Empire apart."

"The Empire is tearing itself apart," Thanos pointed out, but this wasn't the time for that argument. There was too much to think about before any of that. Too much to process all at once. Everything he'd thought about himself had changed. He didn't even know where he fit into the Empire now.

The king seemed to be having as much trouble with it all as Thanos was. He sat there, looking out around the room as though seeking an answer somewhere there.

"I'm glad you know," King Claudius said. "I didn't think I would be. I've spent so long hiding this from you, but now that you know, it feels as though a weight has been lifted from me."

"It's not the only thing I know," Thanos replied. "I know who tried to have me killed."

That brought the king back to his feet again. "You do? Who? I'll have them hanged. I'll have them—"

"Lucious," Thanos said simply.

He saw the change in the king's expression at once. When he'd told King Claudius that he knew the secret of his birth, Thanos had seen pure shock. Now, the surprise was back, but this time it wasn't anywhere near as great. Why would it be? They both knew that Lucious was more than capable of it.

150

"No," King Claudius said, but there wasn't certainty there.

"Yes," Thanos insisted. "He sent a message to the Typhoon, and had him try to kill me. He followed the same clues that I did about my birth, and he wanted me dead because of it. He *wants* me dead."

"Lucious is a prince of the Empire too," King Claudius said, as though that made it impossible that he would do something like this.

"Which explains why he found it so easy to get the Typhoon to do the job," Thanos insisted. "I found the boy he sent to carry the message. Lucious gave him an amulet to identify the message as coming from him."

"And you have this boy? He will swear to this?"

Thanos gritted his teeth. "He was murdered shortly after I spoke with him."

And Thanos thought that the king would have heard of something like that happening in his own castle. Did he really not care what happened to the people who spent their lives serving him?

"He found out what was happening," Thanos insisted. "He sent the boy. Who else could? He should be executed for this!"

"I will not execute Lucious," King Claudius snapped back. "Do not even suggest it."

"Imprison him then," Thanos said. "Put him where he can't do any more harm. You must know what he's like. I thought you were only keeping him around because of his status, but if I'm your son—"

"Lucious has his uses," King Claudius said. "He has a role to play, even if you don't understand it right now."

"What's to understand?" Thanos demanded. He could feel the anger rising in him, overwhelming the strange kind of rightness he'd felt on hearing the king admit who he was. "He tried to kill me. He *did* kill that boy. He needs to be stopped."

"He will do exactly what he needs to do," King Claudius said.

"And you won't do anything to punish him?"

Thanos saw him shake his head.

"Come, Thanos," King Claudius said. "This should be a happy moment. I have a son who knows who I am again. Sit with me, eat."

"Suddenly, I've lost my appetite. Please excuse me, your majesty."

"Thanos," King Claudius said. "Don't do anything foolish."

Foolish? Thanos wasn't going to do anything foolish. He was going to do something he should have done a long time ago. If his newfound father wouldn't do anything about Lucious, then he would.

CHAPTER THIRTY THREE

Lucious liked wine, so it seemed obvious to take a vineyard. When the king had given him license to take what he wanted to show the peasants their place, why shouldn't he?

Not just any vineyard, of course. There were more than enough around Delos producing slop he'd flog a servant for putting in front of him. The Cervin vineyard, though, was worth taking. Not only did it produce wine worth drinking, but its owners sold wine from across the world to every noble Lucious knew. The money from it would be a useful addition to the royal coffers. Lucious would certainly enjoy owning it.

He and his men rode through the fields, probably looking like a band of noble knights out to slay some monster. He saw the workers scatter before them and run. Briefly, Lucious thought about chasing them down for the sport of it, but it was better to do what they'd come to do. They didn't look like slaves, so maybe it was better if they ran, anyway. Lucious didn't want to have to pay workers on his new vineyard.

"Remember what we're here to do," Lucious said, looking around at the men with him. He'd picked them himself, selecting only the hardest, toughest members of the army for the job. He'd wanted men who wouldn't shy away from what was needed. "Let's show Delos the price of rebellion!"

The men roared their response. There had been a couple who had expressed qualms in the last couple of raids. Lucious had ordered them to the front to fight against the rebels there. He had no time for weakness. The men who were left had proven themselves willing to follow any order. Most of them seemed to enjoy it.

They approached the farmhouse at a full gallop, and Lucious casually kicked aside a boy who ran out too close to them, sending him sprawling in a tangle of broken bones. Lucious didn't give him a second look.

The farmhouse was bigger than most around Delos, probably thanks to the money from the wine. It was a hovel compared to the castle, of course, but it wouldn't take much to remodel it for guests or hunting. Perhaps even as a place to keep a noble mistress. He'd had his eye on Stephania for a while now, but there were plenty of others.

Wealthy or not, these people were still peasants, without a drop of noble blood. If anything they were the worst of the lower orders, thinking that the ability to make good wine made them somehow better than all the rest. Maybe even almost as good as those they should serve. Just the thought of that made Lucious glad he'd picked this place.

They stopped outside the door, and Lucious handed his reins to one of the men. He didn't bother knocking, but instead waited while another of his men kicked the thing back against the wall. The man stepped through and Lucious followed.

Inside, he saw a high ceilinged hall, dominated by a long table with silverware set out on it, while a wide staircase stood at the side, hung with trophies the way a noble's home might be. Lucious had been right about these wine makers getting ideas above their station.

There was a fat peasant man with graying hair wearing enough velvet and silver that he could have been a noble. There was a woman the same age, dressed in just as foolish a fashion. A younger man was wearing rough work clothes, but Lucious could see the resemblance between him and his father. There were two younger women, one heavily pregnant and possibly the wife of the young man, the other probably his sister.

The fat man was already rising from the table as Lucious entered.

"What is this?" the wine merchant thundered. "What do you think you're doing, bursting into my home like this? By what right do you—"

Lucious drew his sword in one smooth movement and stabbed the fat man in his ample stomach. He was so huge that the blade didn't even come out of the other side.

"I think I am your prince," Lucious snapped, then stepped back to let the man fall. "And this house is mine now."

"Father!" the younger man cried out. He drew a sickle from his belt, running at Lucious. The blade clattered from the steel of Lucious's armor as he stepped back, then the prince swept his sword across at throat height. He was aiming for a neat beheading, worthy of the warrior he was, but instead, his sword only made it about halfway through the man's throat. He felt it dragged from his hand as the young man collapsed.

"Honestly, can't you peasants even *die* properly?" Lucious demanded. He put a foot on the man's chest and yanked at his sword, only getting angrier as he tried to pull it free. Finally, it came loose.

"You saw them resist," Lucious said to his men. "The families of traitors are forfeit. The young one goes to the slave pits. Hang the others when you're done with them. Find any servants and get them ready to sell if they're worth anything. Kill the others. Then I want this house stripped of anything of value. What are you waiting for? Go!"

His men rushed forward, and the women screamed as they dragged them away. Lucious sat down at the table, enjoying the start of the violence. There was a bottle of wine on it, so he helped himself, drinking straight from it as around the house, more screams sounded. It wasn't the best vintage, but it was more than passable.

He looked around, imagining what he would do with the space as the looting began. The silverware would be worth a decent amount, while the space might be good for parties. Yes, he decided as the body of a servant came tumbling down the stairs, this was a good place to take.

He stepped out into the sunlight, where his men were binding servants on their knees. Lucious strode along the line, silently picking out whether any were worth keeping. One was arguing with his men as they dragged him toward a noose.

"You need me," he said. "Now that the master vintner is dead, I'm the only one who knows all the details of his business."

Lucious stepped in. "Wait. He's right. We do need to know these things."

He heard the servant sigh with relief. Lucious smiled at that.

"So make sure you only kill him once you have beaten every detail out of him," he finished.

He walked on, finding the boy he'd knocked down before. Lucious watched him trying to crawl away, his leg obviously broken, then moved to crouch beside him.

"You might as well stop," he said. "I could catch you any time I wanted."

"Please," the boy said. "Please don't kill me."

"What's your name, boy?" Lucious asked.

"V-Vel."

"Do you know who I am, Vel?" Lucious asked.

"You're Prince Lucious," the boy said.

"And do you know what's happened here?"

"You... you killed them."

"Yes," Lucious said. "Because they were traitors who wouldn't give up what belonged to their betters. Because there is a price to pay for rebellion, and you're all going to pay it until the rebellion stops. It's their fault that this is happening. Do you think you can remember all that?"

The boy nodded.

"Good. I won't have to kill you then. One of my men will splint your leg, and then you can hop your way to Delos. On the way, you will tell anyone you meet all of it, do you understand?"

The boy nodded. "Y-yes."

"Yes what?" Lucious demanded, his voice sharp again.

"Yes, your highness."

"That's better," Lucious said. At least one peasant had learned his proper place today.

It was a start.

CHAPTER THIRTY FOUR

Sartes huddled in amongst the statues and mausoleums of the burial ground, listening to the leaders of the rebellion argue. They'd gathered around one of the slabs there, the map spread out upon it, with Anka at the heart of a cluster of the rebellion's more senior figures. Sartes was that close only because Anka had insisted on it.

"We don't know that they'll come through here, not for sure," a large man who looked like a wharf hand insisted. "We could be committing all our people for no reason."

"Not for no reason, Edrin," a younger man insisted. He looked like a fighter. "To stop the Empire from capturing, torturing, and slaughtering our people."

"You're always taking Anka's side," Hannah said. She'd been at the meeting when they decided on this.

Sartes was starting to get a better sense of who the rebels were. The younger man was Oreth. As Anka struggled to hold the rebellion together, he seemed to be serving as a kind of deputy. The big man, Edrin, was solid but obviously suspicious of whether Anka could do the job. Sartes didn't like Hannah, because it seemed too much like she was more interested in her own place within the rebellion than anything else.

"We're in the right place," Anka said, pointing to the map.

"Then where are they?" another man asked. He was called Yeralt, and Sartes had heard that he was the son of a merchant, probably wealthier than the rest of the rebellion's people. "I don't want to argue, Anka, but our people are getting worried, just waiting like this. They think it's going wrong."

"Then I'll speak to them," Anka said. She looked around, and to Sartes's surprise, he saw her eyes settle on him. "Come with me, Sartes. Let's show them what they're fighting for."

Sartes followed as Anka stepped out onto the road that ran through the burial ground. Around them, rebels slipped out of hiding places in pits and behind statues to listen.

"Listen to me," Anka said. "I know you're scared. I know there are some of you who think that we shouldn't be doing this at all. That we should be running and evacuating our people. The truth is that we could do that." She raised her voice. "We could do that, and the army would march straight through here. It would descend on towns and villages, looking for us, but that would be all right. We wouldn't be there."

"Ordinary people would," Anka went on. "We've all seen what the army can do. It will go into those towns and it will murder people. It will drag them out and torture them. It will conscript young men like Sartes here. It will enslave those who can't fight for them. We could run away, but we won't. We won't, because the people of Delos need us."

That got a cheer from the surrounding rebels, and Sartes couldn't help joining in. Above it, he heard a rumble. Oreth ran up.

"They're coming!"

Sartes saw Anka nod. "Everybody to your places! Remember the plan!"

Sartes ran back to his spot by the statue, and saw the others take up their positions. They practically disappeared back into the landscape of the burial ground once they were there. Sartes watched the approach of the Empire's soldiers from around the arm of a marble figure. His stomach knotted at the thought of what was about to happen, but he didn't move. He didn't run.

Instead, he thought of how brave Ceres would have been if she'd been here. He clutched his sword tighter. His father had made it, and it fit his hand perfectly, in a way that the practice swords the army gave to conscripts never had. In his other hand, he held a horn ready to blow. He wore the uniform that they'd made him wear in the army, because they needed that for the plan.

Around him, Sartes could see the other members of the rebellion. They waited in their hiding places, armed with the armor and weapons they'd started to produce under his father's instructions, positioned exactly according to Anka's instructions throughout the burial ground and the ancient ruins within it.

She stood beside him, and Sartes could see the way she kept her features blank as she tried not to show any fear. She kept looking around, though, and Sartes guessed that she was going over and over the preparations they'd made.

"You didn't miss anything," Sartes whispered. He'd never seen anyone so thorough. "You thought of everything."

"I hope so," Anka whispered back.

Sartes watched the column of soldiers as they got closer. He could see horsemen at the front, armed with swords and short bows, there to serve as scouts or rapidly moving archers. They carried chains on their saddles, and Sartes guessed that they were there to seize prisoners and slaves too. Behind them, he saw the conscripts, easy to recognize in their ragged armor. The regular soldiers followed them, as if to sandwich them in so that they couldn't escape. Sartes could see officers and elite soldiers among them, resplendent in engraved or gilded armor, marked out by red or gold cloaks. At the back of the column came a group in darker colors: slavers and torturers, not there for whatever raid the army was going to conduct, but for its aftermath.

Sartes wet his lips, lifting his horn ready to blow when the time came.

"Not far now," Anka whispered beside him. "Wait for it."

Sartes waited, although that was hard, when the column of soldiers was walking past so close. At any moment, one of the soldiers could have looked round and spotted them, even though they were well hidden amongst the monuments of the burial ground. Any one of them could have seen what was coming and shouted a warning. Then the rebellion would have to withdraw, or risk a much more dangerous battle.

But they didn't look round. They kept going. The soldiers kept marching, the conscripts kept being pushed forward, and Sartes held his breath as the horsemen continued to lead the way.

"Now," Anka whispered, and it almost took Sartes by surprise when she did.

He had to lick his lips again before he could blow his horn, but he managed it. A single high note rang out around the burial ground, and for a moment, everything was still. Then rebels burst from their hiding places ahead of the column, readying bows and firing stones from slings. Sartes saw one hit a horse, so that it reared, throwing its rider from the saddle.

The others drew their blades in response, spurring their horses forward. Sartes swallowed at the sight of the charging war horses and the thundering sound of their hooves. It seemed obvious that they would ride down their attackers, who suddenly seemed too few, and too ill prepared.

Then the horses hit tripwires that Sartes and the others had prepared earlier, and the riders screamed as they fell.

Their horses tumbled, sending riders careening over their backs as they crunched into the ground. Some tried to ride around, only to hit pits lined with spikes. Soon, the riders were trying to leap over their own comrades, and the rebels were shooting at them as they did it. Behind them, Sartes could see the soldiers standing as if they didn't know what to do next.

"Again," Anka said.

Sartes nodded and blew his horn once more.

Now, the burial ground burst into motion. Rebels who had been hiding behind the walls of the ruins pushed at them together using long spars of wood, shoving against spots they had weakened in the night. Stones came tumbling down onto the heads of the soldiers at the edges of the lines, forcing the others to crowd together.

The rebels flung fire pots into the middle of their lines, and they scattered again. Without a solid shield wall, they weren't able to defend against the arrows and stones that rained down on them.

"Now," Anka said, and Sartes blew his horn a final time.

He saw rebels rush from their hiding places. Some rose up from covered pits that looked like freshly dug graves until they struck from them. Others came out of the entrances to the burial ground's catacombs, charging into the sunlight. He saw his father among them, wearing a mail shirt and wielding a hammer large enough to crush through any shield.

All the while, those already in place continued to fire stones and arrows down into the mass of the Empire's soldiers.

Now it was time for Sartes to do his part.

He stepped out in front of them, not knowing if any of them would recognize him. They didn't have to, so long as they listened. He raised his voice over the sounds of the battle.

"Conscripts! My name is Sartes. I escaped from the army to join the rebellion. We are here to rescue you. Join us to fight, or run to safety. You will not be harmed!"

An arrow came toward him, and Sartes dodged to the side, repeating his message. Some of the conscripts looked confused, but at least they weren't joining in the fight while the rebels attacked the main body of soldiers. He saw some break and run, while others threw down their weapons. A few even plunged into the fray, striking at one of the slavers there and dragging him to the ground.

Sartes hung back. Both Anka and his father had been clear on that, but he'd already done his part. Without the conscripts, the Empire's force was far smaller, already crumbling under the assault by the rebels. Taken by surprise, they had no chance to mount a real defense, or reorganize from the long lines of their column into something that could protect their flanks. He saw his father hammering at the shield of an officer, buckling it under the weight of his blows.

Sartes saw a soldier running at him from the battle. For a moment, he thought that maybe one of the conscripts was running to him to get clear of the violence, but the man's sword was out, and he wore the armor of an officer.

"I might die, but at least I'll kill you, traitor!" the officer yelled.

He swung his blade at Sartes, and it was probably ironic that if it hadn't been for his training in the army, Sartes would probably have died right then. As it was, he brought his own sword up, parrying and backing away into the rows of statues.

"You can't run forever, runt," the officer said.

"He doesn't have to," Anka said, stepping in from the side. She thrust a long dagger in past the officer's guard, catching him in the throat. The officer tried to turn to stab her, but Sartes grabbed his arm, holding on until the man fell between them.

"Thank you," Sartes said.

"You're one of us, Sartes," Anka replied. "We look out for one another."

Sartes looked around for another place to help. He saw one of the conscripts who'd joined their side in trouble, frantically defending himself against a pair of slavers armed with clubs. Sartes charged forward.

"This is for my brother!" he yelled, and stabbed the first slaver as he turned. The second swung a set of shackles at his head, then jabbed with his club as Sartes ducked. Sartes cut across the man's leg, then thrust into his chest as he fell.

The rest of the battle didn't take long. With an ambush like that, it was never going to be drawn out, because the rebellion didn't give the Empire's soldiers a chance to fight back the way they were used to. In a matter of minutes, the only soldiers Sartes could see who weren't dead were either freed conscripts or running away.

He looked around at the aftermath of it. He hadn't seen a battle with the army, so he hadn't known what to expect. The reality was hard to look at. There were so many dead bodies there on the ground, piled together so that it was hard to believe that minutes ago they had all been people, walking and breathing. There were dead and injured horses there, brought down by the tripwires, or fallen into pits.

There were members of the rebellion dead too, although there were very few of them, thanks to Anka's plans. Sartes could see injured men and women there, being helped to their feet by their colleagues, and stretchers being brought out of hiding places. Anka had obviously planned for this part too.

It was sickening to see so much death and destruction there. Already, the smell of it was awful, and Sartes knew it would only get worse. It was hard to comprehend the idea of so many people being killed in such a short space of time. Only the thought that if they hadn't done this, these same soldiers would have marauded through a rebel area made it any easier to bear.

"We have to go," Anka said. "Tell the conscripts that they can either scatter or come with us, but they have to decide now. They'll listen better if it comes from you."

Sartes nodded, and stepped out in front of the remaining conscripts to deliver the message. A few more ran off, but the majority stayed. He couldn't decide if that was because they genuinely wanted to join the rebellion, or if they simply didn't have anywhere else to go.

They stood there at the heart of the burial ground, and once more Anka addressed them.

"My friends, today we have won a victory. It has cost us. There is no such thing as a pretty, painless fight. But we must remember what that victory means. It means that young men captured by the Empire now walk free! It means that people who would have been tortured, enslaved, and murdered are safe. Above all, it means that the Empire is one step closer to falling. We have won a victory today, but it won't be our last!"

Sartes was the one who started the chant. It seemed like the obvious thing to do.

"Anka! Anka!"

At first, he was the only one shouting it. Then he heard other voices join his. His father's, Oreth's. The conscripts'. Eventually, the chant reverberated around the burial ground, filling it completely.

They'd found a true leader.

CHAPTER THIRTY FIVE

Thanos was armored for war, and more than ready to kill.

He had his full armor from the Stade in place, his sword at his side, and a shield on his arm. He had a throwing spear strapped to his back and a dagger in his boot. Even his horse was armored, the barding that would protect it from an errant sword stroke shining in the castle courtyard's sun as he tightened the straps on its saddle.

A second horse held his supplies, although the truth was that Thanos doubted this would last long. He would go out, do what was necessary, and return. Or not. Perhaps he would die doing it. Perhaps he would go and join the rebels on Haylon again. It would be hard to come back here after he had killed a prince of the Empire.

"You're going after Lucious, aren't you?" Stephania said. Thanos looked across as she hurried out into the courtyard. Thanos had been hoping to avoid her, if only because he'd known that this would happen, and because she was the one person there it would be hard to leave.

"What are you doing here?" Thanos asked. "You shouldn't be a part of this."

"Did you think you could slip off without me noticing?" Stephania countered. "The servants do occasionally tell me things, you know."

She looked as beautiful as ever, perfectly poised even with a look of worry that seemed out of place with the rest of her. Was she worried about him?

"I'm doing what I need to do," Thanos said.

"Because he tried to kill you," Stephania said. She reached out to put a hand over his as he cinched his saddle tight.

"Not just that," Thanos said. "He's responsible for Ceres's death. He killed that stable hand. Even now, he's out ravaging the countryside, and King Claudius won't do anything about him."

"You can't expect him to execute Lucious," Stephania said. "It's too much to ask."

"He won't even lock him away," Thanos replied. "If you have a mad dog biting people, even if you used to love it, you put it down."

"And you're going to do that, are you?" Stephania shot back. "What if he kills you?"

Thanos had been hoping that Stephania wouldn't ask that question, because there were no easy answers.

163

Thanos forced a smile. "I can outfight Lucious. He's never come close to beating me in a practice match."

"And what if he gets lucky?" Stephania asked. "What about all the men he'll have with him? What if he shoots you with a hunting bow from a nice, safe distance, and claims the rebels did it? He gets to be rid of you and have another excuse to go after them."

"I'll be okay," Thanos insisted.

Stephania stepped between him and his horse. "No you *won't*. Even if you do this, you won't be able to come back. And I want you to come back."

That was enough to make Thanos pause. The sheer closeness of Stephania to him had a lot to do with it, but so did the passion he could hear there in her voice. He could hear how much she cared, and the truth was, he felt the same way. If he could have, he would have stayed there with her.

But wanting something and it being possible weren't the same thing.

"I have to do this," Thanos said. "Lucious has to be stopped. He has to *die*."

"Then we'll make sure that happens," Stephania said. "But there are better ways to do it. Smarter ways."

"What do you mean?" Thanos asked.

He felt the brush of Stephania's hand as she reached out to touch his face, then she did something he'd been dreaming about her doing ever since that moment in his rooms. She kissed him. Her lips touched his, and there was something so sweet about her there that he couldn't help kissing her back.

It was a gentle kiss, a delicate one, there and gone too soon, but it was still amazing. It left Thanos breathing quickly as they parted, and he could see the slight parting of Stephania's lips as she looked at him.

"I need you to trust me," she said. "You *do* trust me, Thanos?"

He nodded. There was no one in the castle he trusted more. There was no one there he cared about more.

"Then trust me to do this," Stephania said, putting a hand on Thanos's chest and gently pushing him back from his horse. "I will find a way. A way that doesn't put you in danger, that means that you can still be here. With me."

That part was hard to ignore.

"I'd like that," Thanos said. He looked at Stephania again. It was so hard for him to take his eyes off her. Every small movement she made seemed to draw his gaze, so that it felt as though the whole world consisted of her. "I was so wrong about you before."

"You were," Stephania said with a smile, "but I'm hoping that you'll have plenty of time to learn everything there is to know about me."

There was something about the way she said it that made Thanos tilt his head to one side. "What do you mean?"

Stephania paused, taking a step back. "I thought… oh, I've got it wrong, haven't I? No, it's a stupid idea. I should have known—"

"What, Stephania?" Thanos said.

She seemed to collect herself. "I thought maybe, with the way you were talking, that you might want to go through with the wedding they planned for us both."

That caught Thanos a little by surprise. He hadn't thought that Stephania might still feel that way after everything that had happened with Ceres. He hadn't dared to.

Thoughts of Ceres made Thanos pause. If she'd still been alive, he wouldn't be thinking like this at all. He would have been trying to save her and be with her. But since her death, he had started to realize how much Stephania really meant to him. Stephania had been the one who was there for him since her death. She'd been the one he'd felt his feelings blossoming for.

"But I know," Stephania went on, "it's too soon, and you have a lot to think about, and—"

Thanos caught her by the arms. "I think that's a wonderful idea, Stephania."

She shook her head. "You're just saying that. You don't have to do this just because you think you ought to, Thanos. You don't know what you're saying."

"I do," Thanos insisted. On impulse, he took one of Stephania's hands in both of his, dropping down to one knee. He wanted her to see just how serious he was about this. Yes, Ceres's death still hurt. He suspected that it would never stop hurting. But Stephania made it feel better, and he wanted this.

"Oh, Thanos, stand up," Stephania said with a laugh.

"Not until I've done this," Thanos said. "Stephania, you've been so good to me, and I've started to realize just how much you mean to me. Maybe if all this hadn't happened, we would have already been married, and right now, I can't think of anything else I want. Will you marry me?"

Stephania paused as if she couldn't quite believe that he'd actually said it. Perhaps she couldn't think what to say. Perhaps she was already having second thoughts.

"Yes," she said, throwing her arms around him. "Yes, of course I'll marry you."

Thanos stood, lifting her up, and Stephania laughed. Right then, Thanos felt like doing the same. Everything else in his life was so complicated, so difficult, but this one thing felt so bright and wonderful.

Stephania was like a point of light in the dark, leading him onward.

CHAPTER THIRTY SIX

Stephania spent the next few hours in preparations, both for the wedding and... otherwise.

She spent most of it considering the joy of marrying Thanos, the dress that she would wear, the feast that would take place, and what it would be like appearing at court on his arm. She worked on how they would announce it to the other nobles, and of course on all the things that would happen afterwards. Her maids and the ladies of the court bustled about her, seemingly delighting in the news even more than she did. In the midst of it all, she sent one with a quiet message.

"Enough of this for now," she said with a carefully exasperated smile. "I think I'm going to walk the gardens. If I'd known that marrying would involve so much, I wouldn't have gotten Thanos to ask me."

They all laughed along with her, of course. Partly, Stephania knew, that was because they'd learned that it was better to laugh at her jokes. Partly, it was because there wasn't a single one of them who could imagine not wanting to marry someone as handsome and powerful as Thanos. Probably a few laughed at her joke that she could make a prince of the Empire do anything.

She had though. The right touches and looks, being there at the right moments... Her show of timidity in the courtyard had been perfectly judged so that he asked her. Stephania wanted Thanos to remember it as his idea, as much as hers.

Now for other business. She walked gracefully along the corridors of the castle, attended by no more than the bare minimum of ladies-in-waiting and noble friends. She smiled and listened to their gossip as she walked, mentally parsing it into the useful and the unlikely easily enough that she barely had to pay attention to it at all.

The talk of Thanos asking her to marry him brought talk of other proposals: the noble girl who was marrying one brother of a family out on the borders while secretly in love with the other, a union between two merchant houses sealed by an arrangement between two nobles still little more than children, a high-born wife who had deserted her husband as he went to war. Stephania made all the appropriate sympathetic noises as they made their way toward the gardens. She carried a wine bottle with her, along with two glasses.

"All this talk has given me quite a headache," Stephania said as they approached. "Might I beg a moment or two of solitude?"

They agreed, of course. No one there was important enough to disagree with anything Stephania suggested, and they knew it. The ones who didn't had been quietly weeded from her social circle a long time ago, or taught appropriate lessons. They probably didn't all believe her about the headache, given the wine, but even those probably only thought that she was saying goodbye to an admirer now that she was to be married. After all, it was what they would do.

It meant that Stephania was able to step into the gardens alone. She had to admit that the palace gardens were beautiful. There was something about the way the blooms hid their thorns that she found particularly appealing.

Her favorites were the long-stemmed white roses, so delicate looking and carefully cultivated that they seemed almost fragile in comparison to other plants, yet more than capable of twisting around them and strangling them if they took up too much space. Stephania reached out to pluck one, ignoring the thorns and lifting it so that she could drink in the heady scent of it.

The man she sought stood at the far end of the garden. He was in his thirties, with slender features and a pointed beard that only added to the effect. His clothes were of high quality, but less grand than those of the best nobles. If Stephania hadn't known what he was, he might have put her in mind of one of those minor nobles who dabbled in poetry or song, using them as an excuse to tour the great houses and court a wealthier wife, engaging in assignations wherever they could in the meantime.

Probably even her maid believed it was something like that. Stephania hoped so. It would be unfortunate to have to make the girl disappear.

"Xanthos," Stephania said, and stepped forward.

"My lady," he said as she came closer. He had a trace of an accent, but Stephania had never quite been able to work out where it was from. Possibly it was feigned, like so much else about him. "Your radiance outshines the sun itself today. You have another task for me?"

Stephania smiled.

"What happened with Thanos?" she asked. "Why did you fail?"

Xanthos swallowed, seeming suddenly nervous.

"I cannot be held responsible for the Typhoon's failures," Xanthos said. "I told you that things would be uncertain within a battle."

He grinned.

"Besides," he added, "it seems to have worked out for the best."

She had to admit he had a point. Things had worked out for the best, after all. Thanos was not dead, but now he was *hers*. And perhaps, after all, that was just as good.

"Perhaps you're right," she said.

She saw him relax and she uncorked the wine, pouring out two glasses. The wine shone clean and pure in the sunlight of the garden.

She lifted her glass. "To success."

"To us," Xanthos countered, and drank his with such speed that it was obvious he wanted to get through this part of it as quickly as possible.

Stephania sighed, and poured hers out into the nearest bush.

"What are you doing that for?" Xanthos asked, and then shocked realization crossed his face. "No, you didn't, you—"

He gagged, clutching his throat and taking a step toward Stephania. His hand fastened on her dress, clutching weakly. Stephania pulled it away. She watched as foam rose at the corners of his mouth, and he fell to his knees.

"I can't afford loose ends, Xanthos," Stephania said. "As far as the world knows, I love Thanos. I have always loved Thanos. I'm sure you understand."

She watched him fall, and stood there, watching, laughing, until finally his body stopped twitching.

CHAPTER THIRTY SEVEN

Ceres stood above one of the island's many bays, feeling the wind ruffle her hair as she stood atop the cliff overlooking it. It felt like there might be a storm coming, but for the moment at least the day was perfect.

She could feel the power thrumming within her, in time to the wind and the rhythms of the island. It seemed to push up against the limits of her skin, filling her in a constant roil of energy that seemed to want to crackle out from her with every touch.

She'd felt the power come to her before, she knew what it felt like, but it had always drifted away again in the past, leaving her feeling ordinary again, human again. Now, it sat there even though there was no danger, and Ceres found herself having to adjust with every movement, accustoming herself to the new strength of her body.

She felt like a different person as she stood there on the cliff edge. Whatever had happened to her after walking through the wall of water, after taking the sacred drink, had changed something within her. It had burnt away whatever it was within her that had been blocking this energy from emerging, had left her moving through the world in a new way. Even the way she responded to it was different

She could feel the wind now breathing against her skin, and the whole island was there behind it if she wanted it. She could understand the islanders' connection to their home now, and the way they tried to fit in with what was around them.

But it wasn't her home, and there were things in the world that were worth trying to change. She couldn't sit back and let the Empire do what it wanted to its people, or let those who ran it get away with sending Thanos to his death. She wanted to see her father and her brother again, too.

Below, Ceres could see the forest folk preparing the vessel that was going to carry her to the Isle Beyond the Mist. They were coming together to craft it, and Ceres could see Eike there among them, joining in where she could. Ceres knew without being told that she wouldn't be taking the girl with her on her voyage. While Ceres had been trying to find a way to control her powers, Eike had found a home to replace the one she'd lost. Ceres couldn't take her away from that.

The way the forest folk crafted her boat kept Ceres watching. Where boat builders back in the Empire would have worked with saws and axes, rivets and tar, the people of the island seemed to be growing a vessel from the living wood of the island. They coaxed and worked, touched the wood and seemed impossibly to stretch it, bringing it together the way a weaver might have spun strands of wool.

They created the boat as Ceres watched, making it rise from the water with smooth, rounded sides and rigging that seemed to be made from creepers. Ceres heard Eoin approaching before she saw him, and the fact that she could hear him when he moved so quietly just showed how in tune with the island she was right then.

He stepped up next to her, and Ceres couldn't help watching him. He stood there with her at the edge, looking as if he could have been rooted in the edge of the cliff.

"It will not be long before your boat is ready," Eoin said. "Our curse has a lot of downsides, but we can work with wood."

"It's incredible," Ceres said. "If you wanted to, you could craft a fleet that could rule the world."

"And why would we want to do that?" Eoin asked. "We're not the Empire, Ceres, to want to rule over others. And we only have so much time in this world, thanks to our curse."

That was a sobering thought. Looking at Eoin there, so strong and so perfect, it was easy to forget that eventually the jungle would claim him as it had claimed so many of the others. Of course he wouldn't want an empire. He had his music, and his people, and that was enough.

"Will you miss me when I'm gone?" Ceres asked.

"Why would I miss you?" Eoin asked with a smile that broke into a laugh at the change of Ceres's expression. "I am with you in spirit."

Ceres's heart rose with those words. She'd thought, in their time on the island, that there had been something there between them. Perhaps if she managed to come back, she could find out.

"I wish that I could journey with you," Eoin said. "But this is a journey for you alone."

Ceres felt a thread of worry at those words. "I don't know the way."

"Your power will set you on the right course," Eoin promised. "You have seen it, after all."

Ceres had, but she'd seen a lot of other things too. She'd seen the violence to follow. And she had seen countless masses chanting her name. Had seen herself as queen.

Queen.

First she had been a slave.

Then a warrior.

And then, one day, somehow, queen.

It did not seem possible.

"Are you ready?" Eoin finally asked, breaking the silence.

Despite all the time she'd spent on the island, it felt to Ceres as though things were moving quickly. She'd expected to have more time. The world seemed to be moving at its own pace, and it wasn't one Ceres was sure she could keep up with.

Even so, Ceres took the first steps down toward the beach. She had a journey to make, and she *did* have to make it. Despite all the power, despite the war, despite everything, only one thing mattered now.

She was going to discover who she really was.

She was going to meet her mother.

COMING SOON!

Book #3 in Of Crowns and Glory

Books by Morgan Rice

THE WAY OF STEEL
ONLY THE WORTHY (BOOK #1)

VAMPIRE, FALLEN
BEFORE DAWN (BOOK #1)

OF CROWNS AND GLORY
SLAVE, WARRIOR, QUEEN (BOOK #1)
ROGUE, PRISONER, PRINCESS (BOOK #2)

KINGS AND SORCERERS
RISE OF THE DRAGONS
RISE OF THE VALIANT
THE WEIGHT OF HONOR
A FORGE OF VALOR
A REALM OF SHADOWS
NIGHT OF THE BOLD

THE SORCERER'S RING
A QUEST OF HEROES
A MARCH OF KINGS
A FATE OF DRAGONS
A CRY OF HONOR
A VOW OF GLORY
A CHARGE OF VALOR
A RITE OF SWORDS
A GRANT OF ARMS
A SKY OF SPELLS
A SEA OF SHIELDS
A REIGN OF STEEL
A LAND OF FIRE
A RULE OF QUEENS
AN OATH OF BROTHERS
A DREAM OF MORTALS
A JOUST OF KNIGHTS
THE GIFT OF BATTLE

THE SURVIVAL TRILOGY
ARENA ONE (Book #1)
ARENA TWO (Book #2)
ARENA THREE (Book #3)

the Vampire Journals
turned (book #1)
loved (book #2)
betrayed (book #3)
destined (book #4)
desired (book #5)
betrothed (book #6)
vowed (book #7)
found (book #8)
resurrected (book #9)
craved (book #10)
fated (book #11)
obsessed (book #12)

About Morgan Rice

Morgan Rice is the #1 bestselling and USA Today bestselling author of the epic fantasy series THE SORCERER'S RING, comprising seventeen books; of the #1 bestselling series THE VAMPIRE JOURNALS, comprising twelve books; of the new vampire series VAMPIRE, FALLEN; of the #1 bestselling series THE SURVIVAL TRILOGY, a post-apocalyptic thriller comprising two books (and counting); of the #1 bestselling epic fantasy series KINGS AND SORCERERS, comprising six books; of the new epic fantasy series THE WAY OF STEEL; and of the new epic fantasy series OF CROWNS AND GLORY. Morgan's books are available in audio and print editions, and translations are available in over 25 languages.

Morgan loves to hear from you, so please feel free to visit www.morganricebooks.com to join the email list, receive a free book, receive free giveaways, download the free app, get the latest exclusive news, connect on Facebook and Twitter, and stay in touch!

CPSIA information can be obtained
at www.ICGtesting.com
Printed in the USA
LVOW04s2050220916
505805LV00015B/146/P

9 781632 918048